Breathless 4:
In Love With an Alpha Billionaire

LOVING MONTIE

by Shani Greene-Dowdell

DEDICATIONS

This book is dedicated to anyone who thinks they'll never find love again.

ACKNOWLEDGMENTS

Thanks to every reader who reached out to me to support this series.
It has been amazing reading your messages and reviews.
I hope this follow-up lives up to the first three books!

Best,
Shani

Justine

I Didn't Hear No Bell

"You really need to see this, Justie."

"What is it?"

"Jacob just purchased a seventeen-million-dollar home for Miss Thang!"

My breath caught in my chest. I was unable to exhale as I registered what Mommy was saying. I had heard through the grapevine that Jacob purchased an elaborate mansion for Destiny and her kids. But why was that bit of news broadcasted in the Miami Herald for all to see?

"That house belongs to you," Mommy's pressured tone cut into my thoughts like a knife. "She doesn't deserve a damn thing. If she hadn't come along, Jacob would be my son-in-law by now..." she rambled on about how Destiny had messed up everything for us.

I hummed to block out the sound of my mother's demanding voice. Sitting in a pear-green, Baroque antique chair reading the morning news, she wore a flawless up-do. Her makeup was picture-perfect. Her back straight as a board, she sat prim and proper in her seat as she talked to me. Everyone bragged about how I mirrored my mother's cover model beauty and trim physique, but I didn't believe them. Why didn't I have the only man I ever loved if I was so perfect?

The man I was groomed to live in matrimony with since I learned my ABCs would soon be another woman's husband.

"I can't, Mommy. I just can't read about him and her," I uttered, unable to say their names aloud, much less read about their newsworthy engagement. "So, please don't keep rubbing it in my face," I pleaded and looked away from my mother in shame.

It wasn't enough that I was hanging onto my sanity by a tiny little thread. To add insult to injury, she was still pressuring me to get Jacob back.

I couldn't stand to listen to her pine on and on about Jacob and the black damsel that swept into his life and became all he needed and more. My parents had arranged for Jacob and me to have a relationship like their own, but that ship sailed, and I wasn't on it. Destiny boarded in my place, and I couldn't do a damn thing about it.

I didn't want to read the headline news. However, I saw it in plain sight from where I sat: *A Fairytale Comes True: Billionaire Jacob Turner Purchases 17 Million-Dollar Home as Gift for Soon-To-Be Wife.*

The headline accompanied a larger-than-life picture of the couple smiling for the camera as Jacob's hand rested just above her hips. They had an entire spread on the power couple, their unconventional love, and the future of his inherited empire.

Without reading the pumped-up drivel, I imagined Destiny doting over Jacob while boasting about her upcoming duties as his wife. She'd probably said something about him completing her. He most likely said she was the love of his life or some other Romeo and Juliet line.

I re-read the headline. *Wife. Wow. She is going to be his wife.*

I intended to kill that bitch to prevent this day from happening. If I had it to do over again, I would squeeze the trigger as soon as she opened Jacob's door. Her shrilling scream and pleas for her life wouldn't affect me if given another chance to end this nightmare.

Murderous thoughts were exactly why I couldn't get sucked back into the world of Jacob and Destiny. Me in their world would be fatal for someone. Thoughts like these rendered me powerless. To know my love for him was unrequited broke a part of me beyond repair. When I felt broken and weak, I wanted to do something to take my power back.

Two weeks ago, I snuck into the expensive home the article bragged about and made love to Jacob one last time. While he may have pretended to think I was Destiny, he knew. How could he not recognize how it felt to touch me inside? She couldn't have possibly snuffed out everything we shared.

Jacob claimed the darkness tricked his eyesight and that he thought I was Destiny. I would never believe it. On my dying day, I would never believe Jacob didn't know he was making love to me. In my soul, I knew he felt me, understood our passion, and needed it again. The familiarity of our love had to have resonated deeply within him.

"What are you going to do about this, Justine?" Mommy's shrilling voice cut back into my thoughts and that savored rainy night when the city lost electricity faded away.

"Nothing...I must get over him to stay positive and find my inner self." I quoted a line from the psychiatrist I had seen since I first caused ridicule for our family by going through a public trial for attacking Destiny and holding her at gunpoint. It should have been enough for my mother that the justice and medical systems thought I was certifiable, but it seemed as if she would push me until I ended up on First 48.

Mommy slammed the paper down and stood abruptly. "No, you need to work some of your magic and get Jacob back! I've been pushing for the two of you to be together since you were toddlers. There is no way Miss Thang has blown in like the putrid wind and taken your future husband. This is *not* happening."

"Mother," I looked at her sternly. "It has already happened. Let it go!"

She rambled on about how she didn't raise me to be a loser and that there had to be something I could do to persuade Jacob that he had made the wrong choice.

Hmmm....mum. I hummed louder to ignore her rant. I struggled enough to hang on to my sanity without her added stress. It was a feat every day not to get up and go slit tires,

8

scratch cars, or kidnap children. With my legal and mental health battles, I didn't need her to keep hounding me about Jacob. I truly didn't think she knew what kind of monster she would awaken by demanding I do something to get him back.

"Well, she needs to go back to that ex-husband of hers. She was slutting around with him after she got out of the hospital. What's his name?" Mommy asked but answered her own question. "Montie. Yeah, Tammy told me all about her sleeping with him. She should've just stayed with him, her own kind. That way, everyone would be better off."

"Yes, ma'am," I offhandedly replied, though I wished there was a way I could ignore her rant. Humming clearly wasn't working.

"And he'll be down here in a few days for that youngest child of theirs birthday party. I hope they rekindle and she realizes she needs to be with him because Jacob belongs to you." Mommy relentlessly dug up old feelings of love, betrayal, and animosity, which resurfaced with a vengeance and swirled around in my mind. My hands shook, and an uncontrollable nervous tick started in my right eye.

She was right.

Jacob had been my lover, friend, and everything to me. He was supposed to be my forever love. Why should he be free while his love held me in a vice grip? Why should I be alone, left with only his memory while he skated off to be happy with Destiny? I deserved to be happy, too.

Only losers roll over and let the other woman win, and I'm no loser, my mind and heart agreed with my mother's rant. "So, the little brat is having a party in two days?" I asked in a devious tone I hadn't spoken in months.

My mother smiled giddily upon hearing me take that tone. "Yes, there will be plenty of guests there, and it should be easy to get close to Jacob then. That might be the perfect time to pull Jacob aside for a heartfelt convincing," she winked, "while Destiny's distracted with the activities of the day." Mommy's face held a scheming grin.

"Hand me that newspaper." I tore it straight down the middle when she handed it to me. I balled up the part of the image that had Destiny in it. "You're right. Jacob is mine, and I have to fight for what's mine."

Mommy handed me a glass of tea. "That's what I want to hear."

I took a sip while glowering heatedly at the crumpled-up paper on the table in front of me as a foolproof plan to reinsert myself into Jacob's life ran through my mind. Two hours later, I parked a block away from his house and waited until a man I was certain was Montie Brown walked out to his car. "He's here already," I mumbled as I jumped in my car and followed him.

Montie would be the perfect weapon in the war I was about to wage against Destiny for Jacob's heart.

Montie

Outside Looking In

There I was in Miami. Destiny planned a big party for Montana.

When we were irresistibly in love, she wanted our creations to be a part of me forever, so she ensured my offspring carried my name. That was then. Now, she had a new fiancée, and I was invited to the massive home they shared as a guest.

In keeping with the truce we made in Atlanta, I interrupted my summer vacation with the kids so Destiny could throw Montana a birthday party.

For the most part, I was unbothered by the intrusion. I arrived in town a day before the party. Destiny wanted to take Montana to the salon and shopping. I wouldn't dare think of my little princess spending her birthday without me or her mother, of whom she was the spitting image. Therefore, I obliged.

What more could a brother ask for than to fly his kids to another state to be with the ex-wife he still loves and her new white husband? Not to throw race around, but damn, was I so bad as a husband that she abandoned the whole race entirely?

After pulling up to their larger-than-life, Italian-style mansion, I shook my head. I hopped out of my rental and received a hearty welcome wave from Jacob and Destiny. They stood inside the foyer, waiting for me to walk up the driveway. It looked like a scene cut right out of a celebrity magazine.

I greeted them with a wave and went inside. I would be fronting if I lied and said seeing Destiny so exhilarated as she walked around showing off her many new possessions with Jacob's hand resting on her back didn't chip away at my soul a bit. Man, it had me lit on the inside.

At one point in my life, my life goal was to share this type of dream home with her. That was when she was my wife, and we were in mutual love. A love I thought we'd recaptured when we reconnected after Jacob's crazy ex attacked her. I thought we were on the road to rebuilding our love while she was healing from her whirlwind infatuation with a white boy. I had no clue this Jacob cat had such a grip on her.

I wrestled with my feelings as she bubbled over with glee, maneuvering about their massive estate. My children ran from room to room, excited about one thing or another. I felt like a grade-A loser, standing on the outside looking in at my family.

I stopped and peered out of an expansive window to allow myself time to bite back the bitterness threatening to rise. If it made it to the surface, I would act ignorant. I didn't want to do that. Not to my children. Not to myself.

I looked to the bright side. My next woman would have the best of me. If I ever found a woman half as special as Destiny, I would never let her go. I would spend my last breath making sure she was living the life of her dreams. I wasn't billionaire status, but my bank account wasn't anything to sneeze at. I had everything I needed and more to spoil the right woman.

"So, man, do you want to hang out later? I'm free to do whatever. How about I show you around the city?" Jacob asked later that evening when we were sitting on the patio sipping a beer.

I had been held hostage by the happy couple most of the day until Destiny took Montana to the mall and thought it would be a good idea for Jacob and me to bond. I was looking for any viable way out. I turned to see Junior swing the racket and hit a tennis ball against the wall as he played a game of solitary tennis on the court about fifteen feet away from the patio. Hanging with Junior was the only positive thing about this 'family day' fiasco.

"Nah, I'd hate to intrude on you and Destiny's evening," I said with a slight tightening of my lips masquerading as a grin. "I'm going to hit a few hot spots up and see what I can get into, solo." I placed my beer on the glass table, which made a soft clank.

"No, no, Montie. You're new to my city. You have to let me show you around," said Jacob. His warm smile had all his teeth showing. Good thing one of us was happy because I felt like smashing something, preferably his big ass silky head.

"I said I'll be fine on my own!" I snapped.

"Cool," Jacob said, throwing his hands up in neutrality.

I didn't mean to pop off on him, but I couldn't think of another way to get him to back down. There was no way I was about to hang out with him. Actually, no way in hell.

"Well, if you don't mind me making a suggestion, I suggest you check out the Lapidus Lounge. Very nice, minimal drama, and high security," he said.

"That's probably what it's going to be then." I stood to offer Jacob a peace offering in the form of a handshake. "I'll be back for the party tomorrow at two," I said.

"Sounds good, man." Jacob stood to his feet, as well. "And Montie, I've been meaning to thank you for being so understanding about Destiny moving here with the kids."

"Yeah," was my reply, but really, what choice did they leave me?

I was past ready to end this conversation. I needed a hardcore drink and a significant distance between me and my ex's perfect little world. It was hard to be happy for them when I thought about her being mine every day. I was the only one left alone in all of this. Who was I going to talk to when I needed a listening ear? Who was going to keep me warm at night?

Except for the love of my children, who would soon be hundreds of miles away daily, companionship was nonexistent in my life.

"No, man, you could've caused a lot of stress through the courts about us moving the kids so far away, but you didn't. I appreciate the way you handled things," Jacob insisted.

"Listen, Jacob, like I said in Atlanta, I just want to see my family…well, my son and daughter happy. I know that starts with their mother," I admitted sternly.

"On that, we can both agree," he said, his eyes widening as he sized up my intent. "Still, I believe one good turn deserves another. So, let me know if you ever need anything for your business or otherwise. I'm here for you."

"That's good to know," I said, doubtful the day would ever come that I would ask him for a damn thing. It was high time this so-called future husband-to-ex-husband bond ended. "Come here, Junior," I called my son over to say my goodbyes.

"Are you about to go, Dad?"

"Yeah, your mom texted me a few minutes ago and said she was on her way back, and I'll be back tomorrow," I told him as I hugged him.

"Okay." He hugged my neck before running back over to the tennis court.

"Take good care of my family," I absentmindedly told Jacob as I watched Junior run off to play. After all we'd been through, I didn't doubt that he cared for them. I just felt compelled to say the words aloud.

"It's already done. You have my word on that," Jacob replied.

"Good then." I turned to walk through the house, unaware of my surroundings this time. I did not look at any of their high-priced possessions. I just wanted out of there.

I passed the maid, almost bumping into her. She rushed ahead of me to open the front door to see me out. "Good day, Mr. Brown," she greeted with a huge, well-paid-for smile.

"Uh-huh." I headed down the steps to my rental. I backed out the driveway into oncoming traffic with a deep pain flowing through me, the magnitude I never would have imagined.

Junior and Montana would be a FaceTime or Skype away. I could fly in and out of Miami with ease. So why did it feel like the breath was being snatched from my body as I left their new home?

Montie
A Stranger in My Arms

I only wanted to focus on enjoying the things available to me: my health, a thriving business, two full-of-life kids, and a relaxing environment with good music, drinks, scantily dressed ladies, and perhaps a good game playing on the big screen. I was ready to infuse myself back into the world of the vibrant and living. Maybe just being around different people would give me a different vibe.

I returned to my hotel and got dressed in black jeans and a gray fitted shirt. An hour later, I walked through the doors of the Lapidus Lounge. I had to admit Jacob was on point suggesting this place. The women in there were top-notch, and the vibe was chill. It was damn near intoxicating. I walked over to the bar and placed my drink order.

"Can I get a shot of Henny?" I asked the tall, lanky bartender.

"Coming right up," the bartender said before turning to grab the Hennessey off the shelf.

"Here you go," he handed me the warm, brown fluid.

I downed it within seconds of it hitting my hands and clanked the glass on the counter. That's when an attractive lady a few seats down caught my attention. Her familiar aura drew me to her. She, too, tossed back shots and stared aimlessly at the bottles on the wall as if she had loved and lost and was somehow searching for fulfillment here.

I guess there really isn't any happiness at the bottom of the glass. She's tossing them shits back and still looks like she's had a crappy hand dealt to her.

After thirty minutes of watching the game on the screen and watching her, I ended our long-suffering. I went to sit beside her.

Well, misery loves company, so here goes...

"Are you here alone?" I asked. I didn't want any problems with any random Miami dudes. A confrontation would only unleash all the wrath inside me on some unsuspecting man.

"It's just me against the world, baby. And now that you're here, it's just me and you," she said with a wink. She took another long swig of her drink, then slowly swayed to the music while in her seat.

"So, I take that as you won't mind if I sit down next to you," I said as I smoothly slid onto the barstool.

"It's a free world," she sang and returned to nursing her drink.

I made myself comfortable beside her. "Care to tell me your name?"

After taking another sip from her drink, her tongue lingered outside her mouth for a few seconds. Her plush, pink lips pouted charmingly as if they held the world's seventh wonder. I imagined all types of things she could do with them to make me forget all about Destiny.

"I'm Tracye."

"Nice to meet you, Tracye. I'm Montie," I said, turning to the bartender. "Give her one more of whatever she's drinking. I'll take a Henny and coke this time."

"Thanks for the drink, Montie. You don't look like you're from around here," she said as she swooshed her blond hair around to the other side of her face.

"Is it that obvious?"

"Yeah," she said with a laugh that I joined in on.

"Well, I'm from Atlanta. I'm here for my daughter's birthday."

"Oh, you have children?"

"Yeah, I have two children."

"Do you have any pictures of them?"

"No, I don't have any pictures with me." I had pictures of my children in my wallet. I just wasn't about to show them to someone I just met – no matter how plump her lips looked on her glass or how nicely her ass spread out across the barstool just beneath her slender waist.

Damn, she's gorgeous.

19

"Well, I bet they are cute if they're anything like their father," she said, giving me a once over.

"Thanks, you're very easy on the eyes yourself," I said, staring at her golden thighs that were easily accessible underneath the short skirt she wore.

I finished off my drink and called for another. I drank until I was nice and tight off alcohol. Conversation flowed effortlessly with Tracye as I savored my third, fourth, and fifth drink over the next hour. When R-Kelly's *Step in the Name of Love* came on, the music flowed from the speakers through me. I felt so nice when I went to settle the tab that I did something I rarely did. I reached for Tracye and pulled her to the dance floor.

"No, wait a minute. What are you doing?" she protested when she realized the direction I was pulling her. "I don't dance," she confirmed with a staggering amount of shock and fear in her eyes. She shook her head fiercely and tugged away from me.

"Just follow my lead. I wouldn't guide you wrong," I assured her.

"Oh my," she said as I pulled her onto the dance floor. At first, she was somewhat rigid. I gave her reassuring smiles, spun her around, and pulled her into my arms. Before the song ended, she grooved to the beat of her own volition, feeling every vibe.

We were still having a bomb ass time three songs later. This was the most fun I'd had since the divorce, besides that short-lived night when I owned every part of Destiny. The night she was all mine. The night I thought I'd reclaimed what was rightfully mine.

"What's wrong?" Tracye asked.

"What do you mean?"

"You stopped dancing," she said.

I stood in the middle of the dance floor, frozen in a daze. "I guess the alcohol is catching up with me. I think I better call it a night," I told her as I walked away from the dance floor, leaving her behind.

"Are you sure you don't want to dance to another song? I could put in a request for whatever you like to dance to," she said once we reached the bar. Her eyes begged for more time, but I was about to bounce.

Tracye tossed back the remainder of the drink she had in her hand and intertwined her fingers with mine. I had lost count of how much she'd drank over the night. I knew the woman was a professional drinker, hands down.

"No, I'm good. I'm about to get out of here," I said, avoiding looking into her eyes for fear that she would know my heart was owned by my ex, who was in love with another man. I don't know why I thought she could read that just from looking at me, but I did. "I have a big day planned tomorrow, with my daughter's birthday party," I said.

"That's right, you told me about that. Well, I guess all good things come to an end," she said, slightly raising her brow. "It was so nice meeting you."

"Same here." I brought her hand that was in mine to my lips. "Thanks for entertaining me this evening. I had a good time. You've really shown me Miami hospitality."

"Well, if you don't mind me being forward," she began.

"Why do I have the feeling you're going to be forward, whether I mind or not?"

"Because I am," she said with a laugh. "But seriously, we don't have to end the night here and now. I'm open and free all night if you are."

I sized Tracye up from her curly blonde hair flowing down her back to her breasts spilling out the top of her shirt to her six-inch stiletto-covered feet. She had a face that put you in the mind of Jennifer Aniston. But her good looks weren't the feature that captivated my senses. My dick jumped in my pants as my eyes raked over her voluptuous breasts and thick golden thighs. Then my verification came with a thoughtful question: Why should I be alone tonight when Destiny is with Jacob?

*****

Twenty-three minutes later, Tracey and I entered my suite. "Would you like a drink, some coffee or anything?" I asked.

"Just shut the fuck up and kiss me already," she said in a demanding rasp.

"Oh, it's like that?" I pulled her to me, and a mutual assault began on one another's lips. Soul-grabbing kisses reached down and snatched up that dormant part of me that I never knew existed.

22

I didn't know where this lady came from, but I had to ensure I kicked her out before morning. Another soul-stirring kiss like the one she just gave me would surely end with me proposing marriage.

She kicked off her shoes and wrestled with taking her clothes off. When she yanked her bra off, her vanilla cream-colored tits sprang toward me, and my dick sprang up, harder than a steel post.

I wasn't a fan of sex with random women, especially one I met in a random city at a random bar. It screamed of desperation. But I needed a distraction from the raw emotions I'd been feeling all day long at Destiny's new home.

I pulled my shirt over my head and unbuckled my pants. By this time, she was completely naked. Her hands ran freely over her body, careful not to miss a spot.

Seeing that I was just standing there looking at her in amazement, she said, "Let me help you with these."

Easing down to her knees, she unzipped my pants and slid them down my legs. I lifted my feet so she could easily slide them off. Once I was free of pants and boxers, she glided her tongue along my legs until she reached my balls. That was when she took my shaft in her hands. Her head swooped in, and every inch of my shaft disappeared into her mouth.

"Got damn girl," I gasped. Her mouth was so hot and so wet. I was about to lose it.

*Shit, shit, shit...*My head flew back as I pumped gently into her hot, pink mouth. I closed my eyes as if the act of closing them would hold this moment of ultimate delight behind my eyelids forever. My hands instantly went to her head to guide her warm mouth as it sheathed and unsheathed my rod in the most erotic ways. She was putting in her bid to be the next Mrs. Brown, and I didn't even know her full name.

"Mmmh," she murmured as she slurped down my precum. And she didn't leave one drop of it behind.

"Tracye..." I said as she made the hottest sounds that were driving me fucking crazy.

Wherever she learned her skills was the real deal. Knowing I couldn't handle her orally much longer without gushing all my goods into her mouth, I backed out of her and held out my hand to help her up.

Standing toe to toe, she looked up at me with the most vulnerable look in her eyes. I reached for her face and brought her lips to mine for a kiss. We kissed so sensuously that I wanted to hold her as close as possible. She looked like she needed shielding from something...like she needed to feel something at that very second. Her vulnerability made us one. I needed to feel something, too.

She ended that tender moment when she jumped into my arms, wrapping her legs around my waist. With her secure in my arms, I backed up to the bed and fell with her landing on top. She repeatedly moaned against my lips as my tongue slid against hers. The more we kissed, the more I felt the urgent need to be inside her. I ground my hips sensuously against hers as I deepened the kiss.

"Condom..." she softly murmured.

I stretched to reach the nightstand and pulled out the box of condoms I bought after having drinks with Jacob. I didn't know if I would even need them but figured it was better to be safe than sorry. I was glad I'd thought ahead.

After applying the condom, she rose and, without any hesitance, slid down my shaft in a slow, gripping motion. She began to ride me gallantly, her wetness slick and intoxicating, as she rocked back and forth. "You feel so good, Montie," she said, sucking my lip up to hers without missing a stroke.

I meticulously hammered into her heat. "No, baby, it's all you. You feel good."

She crashed onto my dick, riding me into a stuporous state of mind. I was determined not to be outdone. I blew out a deep breath and matched her stroke for stroke. Our bodies continuously glided against one another until her moans intensified to groans. She reached behind her and gently squeezed my balls, and a strong surge of energy traveled through my body.

"Come with me," I managed to say, using my last bit of strength to wait for her.

She tightened her grip around my shaft as she rose and fell against me like she was in a rodeo. I couldn't take it any longer. Cum gushed into the latex. She screamed my name and a hundred more expletives as we came in unison.

"I think I love you," I teased once she crashed down on the bed beside me. I was just kidding, but damn. Maybe I could love her. I laughed at the thought.

"Don't play with me. I might take you seriously, and I'm kind of possessive," she said, joining me in laughter.

"You're fucking hot, Tracye," I said, letting out a relaxing sigh. "I'll be here a few more days; do you want to hook up again?"

"I'd like that." Her lips found their way back to mine, and her kiss was again magnetic. She settled her head on my shoulder and nestled it close to me. I held this stranger in my arms, feeling closer than I'd been to anyone in a while. Before long, we were both in a drunken, satisfying sleep.

I could see a trip back to Miami in the near future.

Justine
You're Not Him

I managed to screw Jacob and Montie within the past two weeks, having effectively partaken of Destiny's sloppy seconds twice. I thought it would end with me puking my guts out, but my first time sleeping with a black man was breathtaking. His cock was so humongous that I could hardly take him all in. My eyes went dreamy just thinking about the many ways his thick sword made me call out his name. He was an attentive lover, too. I could get used to the mind-numbing way he peered into my eyes as he stroked me senselessly. Waking up in his wide, muscular arms was just as addictive. But he wasn't *him.*

Snuggled under the weight of Montie's warm body, I thought of Jacob. He had moved his fiancée and stepchildren into our dream home. If I couldn't pry them apart, there was nothing left for me to build with him.

Jacob treated Destiny like a damsel in distress that needed his protection, even after she slept with Montie while Jacob was in Florida sulking over me attacking her. Yeah, my mother had gotten the scoop from Mrs. Tammy, and we were hopeful that he would come to his senses and realize that Destiny was the low-class whore I always knew she was. Yet, the opposite happened.

Destiny convinced Jacob that she was somehow the victim. He accepted her "moment of weakness" and professed his undying love for her. He even gave the bitch a wedding ring as a reward for sleeping with her ex.

Jacob had accepted responsibility for her actions, thinking that his leaving her alone that night to come to my aid was why they'd ended up in that predicament in the first place. What a crock of stinky bull!

Jacob had always been a strong-willed man, but not when it came to *her*. He ate out of the palms of her grimy hands. He was strong with me, but she made him weak.

The truth was Destiny wanted to sleep with Montie, and that was that. Who slips and slides on their ex because something happened that their current boyfriend couldn't control?

Montie shifted in bed, and his grip grew tighter around me. He blew his hot breath on the nape of my neck. The hairs on my neck rose against my will, and an electrifying tinge traveled down my spine. I instantly responded to him as if I was his to possess. Unable and unwilling to accept that he could make me feel that way, I wiggled free from his grasp and got out of bed.

After all, my vanilla-toned body entangled within his chocolate limbs wasn't the picture I imagined would be associated with this feeling of intimacy. But it was a means to an end. The look on Jacob's face when I showed up at his wedding as Montie's plus one would make this scheme worth every minute. He'd probably blow a gasket when he saw me draped on his competition's arm.

Would Jacob want me again when he saw me with another man? Would Destiny get jealous? The thought of flaunting around with Montie like he was mine sent tingling sensations all through me. He wasn't who I wanted, but he damn sure was my best pawn in this dirty game of love and hate.

"Tracye..." he called my fake name, his velvet voice climbing over one side of me and down the other, warming me to my core.

I stood over the bed with my hand cocked to the side on one hip. I stared at his sexy, plump lips as they curled to call out to me.

"Girl, you need to get your sexy ass back in this bed," he roared in a morning rasp. "Stop playing, Tracye."

What was Destiny thinking when she left this man? His strong jawline, thick brows, and tall, hard frame were delectable. Something shifted inside of me as I watched him smile up at me when he called me by my alias. I pushed that reaction aside, refusing to let whatever feeling I had to resonate. I shook myself out of the scene where I forgot everything that had ever been programmed into me and fell for a black guy.

"No, I have a meeting to attend this morning," I lied. I would say anything to get out of the claws of the milk chocolate king lying before me.

He ignored my reply and pulled me down onto the bed. "We're staying in this bed today, so cancel it. I want some more of you."

"No, I really have to go ho—"

He captured the last word within his lips. He reached over to grab a rubber off the nightstand and slipped it over the perfect hunk of meat between his beautifully sculpted thighs.

I should get out of here before...before...

He flipped me over and crammed every inch of mountainous pleasure into my aching hole. And, as he began to stroke my depths, I couldn't figure out why Destiny left this man alone. Jacob was one in a million, but Montie was just as magnetic.

I gripped the sheets beneath me and screamed out his name as he proved to me the many reasons why I hated Destiny. She was privy to two powerful men who knew how to please their women with endless pleasure and both would give the world to *her*.

Montie and I spent an hour making pleasurable memories that would be my dark secret for the rest of my life. I was up getting dressed to leave when I asked, "When are you leaving to go back to Atlanta?"

"I'll be here a few more days. I have my daughter's birthday party today, a rehearsal dinner, and a wedding to attend a few days later."

My ears perked up at the mention of the rehearsal dinner. "Wow, that's a lot going on. Are you in a wedding?"

"No, but I've been invited to enjoy the festivities," he said with sarcasm, and a pained look covered his face.

"What's that look for?"

He focused his attention on me. "I'm only enjoying the view of you sliding on your panties. Is that the look you're talking about?" he asked, and a sly grin danced at the corners of his mouth.

"I see you checking me out, but I was talking about the look on your face when you mentioned the wedding. You don't seem happy about your invitation. Do you want to talk about it?" I pried, hoping he would give me some idea of where he stood on Jacob and Destiny's relationship.

"Nah, I'm good. I just want to get these events over as quickly as possible, so I can get some more of what I really want." He trained his hungry glare upon my breasts as I clasped my bra on tightly.

"Oh, yeah?" I asked in a teasing tone while batting my eyes playfully. "What on earth might that be?" I picked up a pillow and tossed it at him as he stalked toward me. Montie wrapped his arms around my waist and kissed my neck. I struggled free and stared at his charming smile.

"I would love to hang out with you more before I leave. Would you like that?" he asked.

"I would like that more than anything," I said and slid my barely-there skirt up my thighs and over my hips.

Montie's chestnut orbs followed the path of the fabric until I was covered. "I just thought of something," he began. "I don't have a date for the rehearsal dinner or the wedding. Would you like to come along with me?"

"Oh, yes! I'd love to!" I yelled before he could get the full invite out. I jumped up and down and leaped toward him, so excited that he had to think I was a fruit basket. I managed to settle down before I blew my cover. "I mean, I would love to spend more time with you, that is," I said in a calmer tone. I couldn't wait to tell Mommy I'd be crashing Jacob and Destiny's rehearsal dinner.

"Well, good. I'm glad that you're excited about going out with me again. Write your phone number on the scribble pad by my bed, and I'll call or text you with the details."

I gazed into his eyes and pulled his face down by his ears. When our eyes met, I placed a kiss on Montie's lips. A super-sensual moment passed between us as I thanked him for inadvertent assistance in getting my future husband back. All I could think of was reuniting with Jacob. I imagined it was Jacob bestowing such a heartfelt caress against my lips.

He squeezed my butt and pulled me closer to his rock-solid erection. "Mmmm, I really can't wait until we link up again now."

"I can hardly wait myself," I said, skipping over to the pad and writing down my details. "I'll be waiting for your text. I left my number on your nightstand. Be sure to send me the details."

"I sure will."

I blew Montie a kiss and left his suite with renewed faith that I would somehow, someway, be able to get close enough to Jacob to convince him that we belonged together.

Montie
Party Pooper

When she closed the door to my room, all I could say was "damn." I would never forget my first night in Miami, thanks to her. Tracye managed to keep my mind off Destiny the entire night. The sexy blond siren had my full attention and I looked forward to spending more time with her.

I hopped in the shower and got dressed for Montana's birthday party. I donned a fresh pair of black jeans, a brown Polo shirt, and black tennis shoes. I couldn't wait to see my little princess.

When I arrived at Jacob and Destiny's mansion, I noticed Disney characters at the edge of the driveway greeting arriving guests. Larger-than-life animated characters filled the property. Minnie, Mickey, Donald Duck, Dora the Explorer, Doc McStuffins, and more lavished the place.

The sight before me was more than Destiny and I discussed. I guessed I should have been elated, but witnessing an overdone birthday extravaganza for Montana unfold over the next two hours agitated me to no end. I didn't want my kids growing up sheltered, rich, and unable to tell the difference between a blessing and privilege.

It's not that I didn't think Montana deserved the best, but come on, man. No three-year-old needed to have this much hoopla going on that they didn't understand. She was only turning three—not graduating from college.

Did Jacob have to get a skyscraper to circle the party writing her name in the sky every ten minutes?

The gift table was filled with gifts falling off onto the floor. The setting was a long way from the modest life of a hard worker success story I wanted to display to them. I had a tough job keeping my children grounded as it was. This was pile-on. I would keep Junior and Montana humble if it was the only thing I accomplished in raising them—well, co-raising them.

I wished I could say the extravagance was the only thing that had my attention. However, Destiny's mother fawning over Jacob's father was an equal eyesore. She rubbed his face with a towel when he got cake on it. He pulled her off to the side, and they danced to their own music. Destiny was planning a double wedding to include them. Maybe my front row seat to this major event for my daughter was to make it clear that I was old news as husband and son-in-law.

Shaking my head, I turned away from Ms. Clara. I felt so out of place sitting around these people I once knew as my family.

They had moved on and belonged to the Turner family. So, with all that being said, what the hell was my purpose at the party?

Jacob had overstepped his boundary as Montana's stepfather—as if I wasn't even sitting right there—when it came time to cut the cake. He stood opposite Destiny with his hand on my daughter's back, encouraging her to blow out the candles. When Destiny realized I wasn't at the table, she waved her hand, motioning for me to come up and join them. By then, I was sick to my stomach and they had already cut the cake. The glare I shot her way stopped her from beckoning me. It let her know I wouldn't be participating in the showcase as a side dad.

"Do you mind if I talk to Montana and Junior for a second?" I said to Jacob, who hovered over them at the table atop a makeshift stage.

"Sure, man." Jacob stepped aside. "They're all yours."

"I know that," I said for his ears only before saying my goodbyes to Montie and Montana. Jacob acted as if he didn't know they were mine. Destiny was attending to other guests, so I would talk to her later about what transpired at this bougie ass party.

"Daddy, you going?" Montana asked in the sweetest voice that instantly melted the boulder of ice that surrounded my heart.

"Yes, I'm about to go, sweetheart. I'll see you guys soon." I hugged her, and she wrapped her arms around my neck and squeezed as tight as her little arms would allow.

"Are you going back to Atlanta?" Junior asked.

"No, I'm going back to my room. I'll let you know when I get ready to go back to Atlanta," I told him as I rubbed his head.

"Hey guys, look. It's the tooth fairy," Jacob's annoying voice boomed and caught my children's undivided attention.

"Wow! It's the real tooth fairy," Junior ran over to a lady whose face was painted sky blue. She wore light blue leotards and had huge white wings. She hung by strings that were attached to a large float at the edge of the back lawn.

"Fairy, fairy..." Montana said as she toddled over to Jacob and the woman.

"Bye, kids." I waved behind them, then strode from the backyard to the front where my car was parked while looking up flights leaving the city and heading to Atlanta with no stops. "There's no way I can sit through two more events like this. To hell with the rehearsal dinner and wedding. I'll send a gift," I grumbled as I located a flight. I was about to click the button to purchase the ticket when Destiny's name flashed across the front of my screen. "Yeah," my voice roared loud and curt.

"Montie, why did you leave so soon? We were about to do the daddy-daughter dance."

"Didn't look like you guys needed me for anything. Jacob has all the daddy-daughter activities on lock," I barked. "And just in case you don't understand what I'm saying, I don't appreciate that shit one bit!"

"Really, Montie? Are you going to handle it like that? Just leave in the middle of the party?" Destiny sounded dumbfounded.

"Yeah, really. I'm not here for it if this is what it will be like. You're not going to have me watching while you let my children think he's taking my place. No, especially not when I'm sitting right there. I thought we talked about this already. You guaranteed me that this would not happen."

"I expected you to come to the stage when I announced we were about to cut the cake. Instead, you just sat there drinking your beer like you don't know what your place is. Jacob stepped in like he should when the father isn't present, mind or body. For this to work, you'll have to meet us halfway, Montie."

I considered that maybe I was half jealous and half an asshole when I sat off to the side and watched Jacob step up for me. So, I gave her that point. I could have easily taken my rightful place by Montana's side. I never had a problem with it before. But my attitude ranged from understanding to jacked up regarding the new stepfather role in my family.

"Well, I left because I didn't want to cause a scene. Even if I give you the point that I should have gotten up, you know I'm here, Destiny. The summertime is my time with the kids, so coming to Miami early only happened because I approved of it. For you to act like I'm not there has me feeling some type of way that I don't care to explain right now. For that reason, I'll have to celebrate Montana's birthday separately."

"Montie, you feel some way because you can't stand to see Jacob in a good mood and trying to do his best for our kids. You want to be the only one they want or need, but you must get out of your feelings and realize that we have a new family dynamic. Step up to the plate and take your place."

"I'm not in my feelings." I flat out lied. I felt more for Destiny than I'd ever felt for another woman, and my two kids were my beginning and end. Of course, I was in my feelings.

"Remember, I know you better than most," Destiny cut into my thoughts. "I know exactly how you feel right now."

"You should know me. We promised to love each other forever. You were my *wife*."

"Yes, that's why I know today you feel like an outcast." There was a long pause where the line was silent as we sat there, listening to each other breathe. "That's why I called you. I want you to always know that we're the original four—me, you, Montie Jr., and Montana. When caring for our children, we must always be in a good place, okay?"

"This is not the good place I want for us. I thought I could deal with it, but no, not like this. I want my family back," I poured out the contents I'd been keeping locked away in my soul. "Every day, I hope I'll wake up, and the past few years will be a nightmare that I finally shook."

"Montie, we can't go backwards. This is the way it has to be," she said.

"Why did you really call me?" I asked, not understanding why she continued to taunt me with a truth I had yet accepted.

"Because I care about your feelings, and I just—"

"If you cared about my feelings, I mean, really cared, you would have waited on me."

"I can't believe you're going there right now. After all we have been through, you still lead us back to our past. What did you think I was supposed to do, sit around and wait on you to decide that you wanted to be a husband? You know what, I don't even know why I'm entertaining this. I have to go," she said in a low, winded tone.

"You're *entertaining* it because it's not our past. It hasn't been that long since I made love to you. If I sit still long enough, I can still feel you all over me."

Destiny gasped. "Montie, let it go. Just be there for our children."

"If you can let us go so easily, I think it's time for me to ask if you ever loved me in the first place."

"Of course, I loved you." She paused. "But our time has come and gone. Our ship has sailed."

"It doesn't have to be that way, Destiny. You haven't married him yet, and if you look around, you'd be able to see our ship has come back to the shore. It's just waiting for you to get on. Everything I have ever had to offer is still yours for the taking."

"No! I can't do this. I didn't call to discuss our past."

"Destiny—"

"I'll talk to Jacob about stepping back when you're here because it's only right, but I'm marrying him."

My heart dropped out of my chest. I felt empty. "You don't have to tell me how you truly feel about me. I know. Just make sure what happened today never happens again, and I'll be fine with that part. I can't see myself getting over losing you, however."

"I'll make sure it doesn't happen again," she said without addressing the divulgence of my feelings for her.

"Good, because while I can't officially claim you as mine like I want to, Junior and Montana are mine by blood."

"No one is denying that."

"Then, we shouldn't have to have this conversation ever again. When I am present, and someone asks for their father to step forward, I. Am. The. Only. One. Who. Should. Step. Forward."

"Understood, and I'll talk to him. But he cares about them too." She sighed. "Are you still coming to the rehearsal dinner? And before you answer, I need you there to show our kids their parents are in solidarity with me marrying Jacob."

"I'm not in solidarity with you marrying him, but I'll be there since it's what you want." I ended the call, and the flight itinerary popped back on my screen, with thoughts in my mind of whether I should leave or stay.

Justine

Revelations

"I'm glad you came with me. I didn't want to go to this shindig alone," Montie said as we pulled into the parking lot for the reception hall.

"Of course. I'm glad you called and gave me the details. Even though you said you wanted me to come with you to the rehearsal dinner, I thought after our night at the hotel that would be all she wrote about us."

"I told you I would call you," Montie's velvety tone filled the car, causing me to smile.

In an alternate world, another time-another place, I would take him out of his misery of pining for Destiny and love him back to life. She was cruel to him for dumping him and then asking him to watch her commit to another man. It was as if she wanted him to be complicit in breaking his own heart. Let's not mention that she dragged his precious little ones along to his torture.

"Men say they're going to call all the time. I'm glad you called," I admitted, hoping we could be allies in getting what we both wanted most...our true loves. The ones meant for us.

"Well, I'm a man of my word, Justine." He looked at me, and I smiled at him. "I have plans for you after we leave tonight," Montie said, staring at my plum red gloss-covered lips.

The last time we were together, he constantly watched my lips before his eyes traveled down my body and stopped at my most intimate places. Why did men use me for what they wanted and then move on and put a ring on the next woman?

"I bet you do have plans, Mr. Montie. You men are all the same," I said, knowing full well that after the disclosures of this night, the last thing he would be thinking about was his "plans" for me.

"What do you mean by that statement?" he asked with a slight frown. "I'm my own man and not like any other."

"Well, you would be the first for me if you're different. I know how the guys are that I have been with. They want their cake and someone else's cake too. Montie hadn't told me whose dinner we were attending, so I vaguely stated, "The guy in there probably isn't even true to the woman he's about to marry." I pointed to the door.

"You don't know me well enough to stereotype me as every other man in the world. You don't know the man inside the building that's getting married, either. So, explain why you think all men disrespect their women solely because you dated a few creeps."

43

"Well, I know that I was able to sleep with my ex not too long ago, and he's about to get married. As a matter of fact, he's having his rehearsal dinner tonight somewhere in Miami. He's probably going to look his fiancée in the eyes and tell her that she's the one for him, knowing he made passionate love to me in their big mansion only weeks ago. So, don't tell me about men when most of them don't even respect their engagement," I blustered.

"Woah, what about *your* responsibility in the situation? You didn't have to sleep with an almost married man," he chuckled. "You could have respected their engagement, too."

"Humph! That's what you say. I love that man because he was mine to begin with. I don't feel like the other woman when I'm with him," I stopped short of saying I was and would always be Jacob Turner's woman. I wanted to make it inside the event, so I needed Montie's invitation to hold. I was on a mission. "Besides, if a man loves a woman, he doesn't cheat. I didn't cheat. He did," I added in a more subdued tone.

"Well, you have a point there. One thing I never did was cheat on my ex-wife," Montie admitted. I nearly gagged at the mention of Destiny. "She was the only woman I ever wanted to make love to," he added, and the faraway look in his eyes told me he was envisioning him and her together, making the sweetest love.

"If it's true that you only had eyes for her, you're one of the good ones, Montie. Too bad she couldn't see it when you were together," I said.

He nodded, stepped out of the car, and opened my door. "Look, I've loved and lost, Tracye. It seems like you've done the same thing. Maybe we can just enjoy each other's company and try to forget our past loves for the next few hours. Deal?" he asked, holding a hand out to me.

"Deal." A counterfeit grin splayed across my face as I intertwined my arm in his. He fell for it hook, line and sinker. As soon as he figured out my ex was Jacob, he would also realize Jacob was the engaged man I slept with. He would tell Destiny everything to get her back in his arms. Then Destiny would know Jacob wasn't beholden to her like she thought he was. Jacob would be shattered when Destiny left him, and I'd be waiting to put him back together again. My plan would reposition all the players, and I would get what I desired.

Humph...loved and lost? I'm no loser. I will win when Jacob realizes he still loves me and Destiny returns to Montie. So really, everybody wins.

I looked at Montie. He returned my gaze with a question in his prominent brown eyes. His kissable dark lips pointed in my direction. He wanted to say something.

"What?" I asked, having gotten sidetracked by my thoughts.

"I want you to enjoy yourself and forget about that loser, aight?"

"Alright," I said and stopped walking. I squeezed his large hand into mine. "I have to tell you something, Montie. I don't know how to say this, but earlier in the car, it may have sounded like I was saying you're not a good man. That's not what I meant. I was just saying I believe some people are who they are." Montie nodded and I continued. "I mean, look at you. You're a successful, sexy man and we took a spin in the bed on the first night within hours of meeting each other. Who's to say you're not engaged to some unsuspecting woman in Atlanta? Or that you don't have a woman somewhere daydreaming about the things you did to me, just waiting for you to come back and make her whole again?"

"There is no one to say those things about me. I'm not engaged and I don't have a woman. You don't have to believe it, but I'm a one woman's man. I always have been and always will be."

"Ha! My ex, who threw me out of his house a few weeks after sexing me down, said the same thing. He went as far as to pretend he thought I was his wife as we made love. Raindrops were beating on his million-dollar home, and we kissed each other like our lives depended on it as he stroked inside me. It was more than he says...."

Montie held his hand up, ceasing my rumination about the last night I got touched by Jacob's loving hands. "Hold up. That's too many details." He looked sickened by the ways that Jacob took me. However, it was the same way he planned to use me after we left this party.

Whatever.

After the fiasco I planned to create at the wedding rehearsal, Montie's last thought would be sleeping with me once it was all said and done. Oh, I couldn't wait.

A devious grin spread across my face as I imagined the moment this façade of Tracye would come to a head. The game I was playing was going to land perfectly.

Destiny was about to discover that I made love to Jacob in the seventeen million-dollar home people were boasting about all over town. Montie would be stunned. Destiny would be crushed. Jacob would be upset, but he would come around. And I—I would have my revenge and my man.

Montie
Bittersweet

Don't get me wrong, being with Tracye took my mind off Destiny. Well, until the woman of my heart, all the woman I could ever need and want, stood only feet away from me. If only I knew what she really needed when she was mine. I had tunnel vision, clouded by the drive to succeed. Success came to be something I regretted and loathed because it cost me my family. In my mind, I thought once I turned my company into a six-figure a-month success, I'd be able to kick back without any financial worries and live larger than life *with* my family.

Like any successful business, my company became a leach, sucking the wind out of my world. Before I knew anything, I was waking up every morning and getting dressed without speaking to my wife and kids. I'd get home late at night, don my pajamas, and do more work before crashing at my computer. That was it for years, the years she needed me to be by her side with our new babies. I understood what she meant when she said I left her a long time before she left me. That understanding hurt like hell.

In a few days, another man would make her his. A man who had his fortune handed to him, so he had the time to win her heart and keep it. He never knew a day of long, hard work to make something out of nothing. Yet, she was about to vow to spend the rest of her life as his wife, and, for some twisted reason, she wanted to do it with me as a witness.

I'd been lured into sitting there and watching another man claim my woman, a fact I had difficulty reconciling. I'd been a good sport, but how much can a brother take before he breaks?

Whenever I pled my case to Destiny, she would shut me down. Loverboy came in and sewed her heart so tight that it's seemingly impenetrable. When his friend attacked her earlier this year, she let me back in and I had the time of my life. That night of being one with my heart, dancing with her soul and ravishing her succulent body taunted me to this day...

"Damn, baby," I grunted against her lips. She was tight...and hot...and tight. Fuck! I missed the feel of her like hell. I had slowly thrust my full length inside her, slamming against her tight walls. I wanted to take it slow and appreciate every moment we had together, but when her hips began to move and meet my thrusts, I rocked her core with an untamed pounding.

The urgency was my trying to show her that we needed that moment. She had moaned salaciously against my lips—a sound so precious to my ears—as our hips picked up speed and rocked against each other, causing more pleasure with each heated thrust.

It was a night I'd never forget. What I wouldn't give to be inside of her again.

I sucked in a deep breath to tamp back my desire for Destiny. As I relived that revered night, my soldier stood high in my pants, ready to make his introduction to a room full of unsuspecting people at the rehearsal dinner.

A vanilla arm intertwined with mine contrasted with my reverie. I smiled at my date. She was a beautiful woman who would find someone to love her if she could let go of the pain inside. But who was I kidding? I knew firsthand that life after pain was easier said than done.

Letting go of my family was the hardest thing I ever had to do. In all the days of my life, I will never forget the day Destiny asked me to leave our old home. It was symbolic of her removing me from her life and choosing Jacob.

"So, it's just like that? You want me to leave so you can talk to him, Destiny?" I stared Jacob down.

"Yes, Montie, I do." It only took four words to wipe out all the years of blood, sweat, and tears I put into building the very home we were standing in.

"Excuse me?" Tracye asked, bringing my attention back to the present.

"Huh?"

"What did you say earlier?"

"Oh, I was just going to say let's enjoy each other tonight. We're all we got right now," I joked outright, but the sentiment was dead on.

"Deal," she said and laughed. "Right now, we're all we got."

Jacob and Destiny practiced their entire ceremony, including their first dance. The wedding coordinator covered every move they would make several times until he was satisfied the event would be worthy of being called a royal affair.

Tracye and I stood idly by in the immaculately decorated hall with a mixture of cream and gold color schemes.

After the stress of watching the woman I loved perfect her plans to unite with another man, I was glad when Jacob left her side. He walked over to the hors d'oeuvre table to get something to drink, giving me a moment with the most beautiful woman in the room.

"You look lovely, Destiny."

"Thanks, Montie."

I knew she didn't want me to, but I couldn't help but ask one last time. "So, you're really going to tie the knot again?"

With another man?

"I am, and it means a lot to have you here. Thanks for coming, Montie," she said while holding an ambiguous smile. "I want you to be happy for me," she added.

I took a deep breath and scanned the room to gather the renegade thoughts running through my mind. I saw Tracye standing beside Jacob, talking to him. They were engaged in an energetic back and forth. Knowing her, she was

51

keeping him busy with small bubbly talk. Ms. Clara and John were in the middle of the floor, dancing to *Made for Love.* Hundreds of guests mingled, ate, or danced to their heart's content.

"You really look beautiful, Destiny," I complimented as my eyes roamed over the cream pantsuit, hugging her curves for dear life. I couldn't hide my desire to touch her one last time if I wanted to. And I didn't want to hide a damn thing. "Do you mind if I get one last hug before you tie the knot?"

"I'll do you one better." Destiny's hips jiggled as she walked toward the door. She peered over her shoulder to make sure I was following.

Damn right, I was. I shadowed her out of the reception hall into the dimly lit hallway, where she wrapped her arms around my neck as soon as I stepped over the threshold. I leaned down to pull her close and accept all the love she was willing to give. She hugged me tightly, allowing her body to connect with mine. Why couldn't she see that she fit so perfectly? We were made to be in this love together.

"I love you, Montie," she said as she stared nostalgically into my eyes. I might've been wrong, but I saw her realize the sacrifices I made for our family. I saw her appreciate them. Most importantly, I saw her love for me. "Always will love you, no matter what. I just want you to know that."

"I love you too, Destiny. Why do we have to be apart?" I had to ask.

She touched my lips. "Don't question where we are. We may not have worked out, but you are a good man. I pray every day that God sends a great woman to you."

"But you are gr…." I started to say more, but she lowered her fingers and grazed my lips with a loving kiss. It wasn't erotic, but it was mind-blowing, just the same. My eyes closed and I took in her essence as her lips slid across mine. Our hug broke, and the heart-bonding contact was gone as fast as it came. The look in her eyes revealed that she still cared deeply for me, but it wasn't the kind of love that would bring her back to me.

A tear slipped from the corner of her eye. "Thanks for showing me what love is and what it isn't, Montie. I promise to be the best mother to our kids and to keep you involved."

"Destiny," I began, but she held up a hand and backed away from me, walking towards the ladies' bathroom.

"I have to go," she said as she fanned her face. "My makeup will be messed up if I start crying."

Following her into the ladies' room and reminding her why I was the best man for her crossed my mind, but only temporarily. I touched my lips, remembering the softest and sweetest lips I ever had the privilege of tasting had been there. I stepped back into the reception hall to find Tracye. This was it. I was leaving Miami and Destiny behind me. I couldn't keep this tug of war with my heart going any longer.

"Stop it! I said I'm here with a date, Jacob! I'm Montie's plus one," a woman's voice yelled, bringing my attention to a screaming Tracye.

What the hell….

"Is everything alright out here?" I asked, curious as to why Tracye was standing near the exit door, yelling at Jacob.

"Everything is just fine, Montie. I just didn't know we had the same *friend*," she said with a quick smile in Jacob's direction. "Thank God you found me out here. Where were you when I was looking for you earlier?"

I looked between Tracye and Jacob suspiciously. "I would introduce you, but I see you two have met. How do you two know each other, and why were you yelling, Tracye?"

She didn't answer that question as readily as she did before.

Jacob blew out a deep breath but remained silent also.

I patted the man—whose shoes I'd give anything to be in—on the shoulder. He would have a front-row seat watching my son grow into a man and my daughter grow into a lady with the finest woman by his side. He was the biggest winner tonight.

"Jacob is the big cheese here in Miami. You obviously know each other already," I provided an answer that should suffice since they were both oddly tight-lipped.

"So, you told him your name was Tracye?" Jacob asked in a dry tone.

Confusion crept up on me, and my sarcastic smile faded away fast. "Yeah, that's what it is, right?"

"Unfortunately, this is the woman that attacked Destiny. This is Justine, my old friend."

"Ex-girlfriend," Justine corrected, and every ounce of cool left me.

No fucking way. She couldn't be Justine. "The one who put Destiny in the hospital?" I asked and turned to face her.

"Yes, that Justine," Jacob clarified.

"What kind of game have you been playing with me?" I yelled, and my fists tightened into a knot instinctively. I'd never hit a lady, but this bitch had assaulted the mother of my children.

"Montie, I haven't been playing with you. This was never about you." She looked at Jacob but reached for me.

"To hell, you haven't been playing. You told me your name was Tracye, and I was stupid enough to believe you!" I pushed her arm away and shoved her when she tried to touch me. I didn't have a record of hitting women, but she deserved a special kind of smacking for hurting Destiny.

"I didn't tell you my real name because I was afraid you would judge me before you got to know me. As oddly as it sounds, what happened between us was real as far as our connection."

"You know what; I don't want to hear anything you have to say. I would never knowingly bring anyone around the mother of my kids who tried to hurt her," I growled, then turned to Jacob. "I meant no disrespect bringing her here. She's crazy," I said somberly.

"Montie, man, I know you didn't mean any harm. Justine is a conniving, cold piece of work. Now, get out of here, right now, Justine!" Jacob yelled as he looked her icily in the eye.

"You would know how cold my work is better than anyone, Jacob," Justine insinuated more than she said.

Jacob wrung his anxious hands together. "I know that you better get out of this reception hall."

"Montie, will you let him talk to me like that? I'm still your invited guest."

"You should call a cab and get out of here, Justine, Tracye or whatever your name is! I'm done with this!" I waved my hand and walked off, leaving Justine standing with Jacob. I stormed away from the rehearsal dinner, having had a moment of affection with Destiny that I would forever treasure and a hate-filled revelation about Tracye, well, Justine's deception.

"Dammit. Dammit. Dammit. Dammit!" I flung my car in reverse and skidded backwards into the dark parking lot. I yanked the car into drive and sped through the neighborhood. "I'm done with it all!" I yelled to the empty compartment of my rental car.

Justine had caught me up in her trap. Jacob's ex-girl had seduced me and came along as my guest to their rehearsal dinner. *Was she still trying to hurt Destiny?*

I rode a few more blocks, my mind rewinding through the Miami trip: my plane touched down, my arrival at Jacob's house, us having a beer, going to Lapidus, sleeping with Justine, inviting her to the rehearsal dinner, the birthday party, and then tonight. That's when it hit me.

Justine said she slept with her ex, who was rich and had his rehearsal dinner tonight. She told me before we entered the building that she had slept with him recently. My stomach fell into my groin. Jacob had taken Destiny from me and was still banging the woman who damn near killed her.

Justine couldn't be trusted, especially since she tricked the hell out of me, but what gives? What if she was telling the truth about sleeping with Jacob?

"No wonder he wanted to move my family to Miami. It's a threefold win for him. He's close to his business, close to his mistress, and Destiny is far away from me," my thoughts flowed through my lips as I drove down the highway going ninety to nothing.

I headed back to my hotel room. I got all my things jam-packed into my suitcase, checked out, and sped off to the airport. I was hopping on the first thing smoking back to Atlanta. Forget the wedding and reception and double-dog fuck Miami. I would plan for the remaining summer with the kids later. Right then, I needed distance between myself and all the foolishness going on there.

After checking my rental in, I boarded my plane. What kind of person did Justine think I was? What kind of person was she? How did I get caught up?

Justine sat at the edge of that bar begging for attention. I offered it to her to receive the much-needed affection I needed in return. We had a damn good time. When I invited her to the rehearsal dinner the next morning, she nearly flipped over to the piece of paper to write down her name and number. Now that I played that back a second time, I realized just how cold the setup was. When we pulled up to the banquet hall, she didn't have to mention sleeping with her ex, but she wanted to make sure I knew about her and Jacob.

"Wow! I believe her. She screwed Jacob since he's been engaged to Destiny," I stated, convinced.

"Who screwed Jacob?" the 40-something man sitting next to me asked, with a sincerely alarmed look on his face, alerting me that I was talking aloud.

"My bad. I didn't mean to talk out like that," I said as I sat back in my seat.

The man shrugged his shoulders and went back to reading his newspaper.

When we finally started rolling down the tarmac and the engine roared and lifted us into the sky, I felt my first moment of peace. I laid my head back on the headrest and blew out a long gush of air from my lungs. No more Jacob, Destiny or Tracye—or Justine—whatever her name is, at least for a while.

I desired to clear my head, and I did as I drank one bottle, two bottles, three...of the miniature vodkas provided on the plane. Once I was nicely zooted out of reality, I played some music. I rode the rest of the ride home quietly.

*****

When I got home, I immediately called up my closest homeboy to run the events of the past twenty-four hours by someone outside of the situation. Mario would keep it one hundred with me.

"Mario, man. What's up?" I asked.

"Shoot, man, you got it. I'm just sitting around here thinking of something to get into. What's up with you, Mont?"

"Man, you wouldn't be able to figure out what's up with me if you had stood beside me the whole time I was in Miami. That's how crazy the past few days have been."

"Whoa. Sounds heavy. What happened, bro?"

I decided to start from the beginning and break down the entire weekend play-by-play. "Well..." I sighed and sat back in my recliner. "It started with me having to watch dude walk around his fancy house with my wife on his arm."

Mario cut in. "She's technically not your wife anymore. When are you going to stop calling her that?"

"I know what we are technically, smart ass. But you also know how I feel about that woman. She'll always hold that title to me."

"Yeah, that'll change when the right one comes and takes it from her." He was always talking sensible, trying to get me to move on, while I was dead set on the facts as I wanted to see them.

"There's no other right one for me, but that's not what I called to talk about," I said before Mario could say anything else.

"Okay, bro, what happened?" he asked.

"After dealing with their displays of affection and their larger-than-life lifestyle, I had enough and went out to enjoy the festivities of Miami alone, if you know what I mean?"

"Now, that's what I'm talking about. What you get into?" Mario perked up.

"You will never guess."

"No, that's why your bonehead is gonna tell me." He laughed.

"I got your bonehead the next time I see you," I joined him in laughter. "No, but in all seriousness. The woman I met and took back to my hotel room was that white girl, Justine...Jacob's friend."

"The one that attacked Destiny?"

"The one and only."

"You've got to be shitting me. Bro—"

"Here's the kicker. We hung out my first night there and hit it off pretty good. I hooked up with her again as my date to the rehearsal dinner...."

"Not knowing who she was at the time," Mario finished my sentence with me. "Awe, man, that's jacked up."

"But check this out. Right before we went into the dinner, she told me she had just slept with her engaged ex a little over a week ago in his mansion."

"Wait, so she's saying she slept with Jacob recently?" Mario sounded puzzled.

"Yeah, that's what I think happened. There's no other way to put her story together but to conclude that she slept with Jacob. If you had seen how he argued with her out in the hallway at the rehearsal dinner, you would have automatically known that they had something going on, still. Putting it all together, tell me what you think."

"This is like some *Young and the Restless* meets *Housewives of Atlanta* meets *Love and Hip Hop*. Wait a minute, I know you answered this, but it's a lot to unpack. Did you say ol' girl was the same girl that held Destiny down at gunpoint? The same one that also said she has been sleeping with Jacob? The dude that's marrying Destiny?" Mario asked, seemingly unwilling or unable to believe the bizarre story.

"Yes, yes, and yes."

"This is a lot."

"You're telling me that it's a lot? I'm the one who has to deal with it."

"It looks like Karma is making visits, and she does not forget anyone," Mario warned in a low, pensive tone.

"Yeah, since Jacob is a scum bucket parading around like a saint, he will get his Karma soon. He's about to marry Destiny, but he's been cheating on her. When she finds out about their affair, which I'm almost certain she will with Justine walking around free to wreak havoc, it will destroy my family again. Too bad his bad Karma is indirectly good and bad for me."

"I don't know about this Justine chick. She has an agenda of her own. You might want to figure out what it is before you get too optimistic about your future with Destiny," Mario said sarcastically.

"I hear you talking. What're you saying, though?"

"Well, first, she hooked up with you on a humbug. Then, she made it a point that you knew she'd slept with Jacob. If she wanted, she could have already blown up the city with her secret, but instead, she coincidentally ends up in your sack and tells it to you. I call foul. I just don't know on who."

"Justine's foul, and Jacob is too, for real."

61

"Yeah, but Justine is up to something else with all this sneaking around and passive-aggressiveness. I've had my share of unstable women. It just doesn't seem like it's her MO to be subtle. She's already physically attacked Destiny."

"I can't start thinking about the hidden agenda, Mario. I'm still decoding the obvious."

"Yeah, well, women can be catty but very meticulous too. Her mess may take months to decode," Mario offered.

"You might be right about that. She wouldn't let us walk into the building until she told her story about sleeping with her ex. Then, I get in there and find out it's Jacob."

"Maybe he slept with her in retaliation for you and Destiny sleeping together. We men don't get over cheating easily. A man used to having his way like Jacob is probably worse," Mario threw in.

"He'd better not be fucking around my family because of his ego. The only reason I gave my blessings for her to move my kids to Miami was that she convinced me of how good he was to her. I didn't want to get in the way of her happiness since she was hell-bent that it couldn't happen with me. She claimed the ol' boy was a safe choice to be around my kids, but if he got all this damn drama coming his way with that crazy bitch involved, I don't think so."

"Well, all you can do at this point is keep your eyes open and stay out the way."

I let out a strained breath. "I know that's what I *should* do, but after Destiny kissed me tonight, and I found out about—"

"Wait a minute. She kissed you?"

"Yeah, but it was more of a 'thanks for letting me go,' goodbye kiss."

"Uh-huh."

"It shook me up and finding out this mess makes me want to tell her to save her from marrying the jerk. I just don't want to look like a troublemaker and have it backfire on me."

"And a troublemaker is exactly what you will look like." We both pause on the line, thinking. "Man, look, it's not your place to reveal her fiancé's unfaithfulness. Y'all have already been through this anyway. It's a replay in reverse. You slept with Destiny; Jacob forgave her. He slept with Justine. What do you think she's gonna do for him?" He didn't give me a chance to formulate an answer. "She'll forgive him like he did for her, and you will be stuck looking like the bad guy for trying to break them up."

"But don't you think she deserves to know? Jacob knows about what we did, but he gets to walk around like his hands are clean," I argue.

"What's done in the dark will come to light. You don't even have to worry about it."

"You're right about that," I said, sounding half persuaded.

"In the end, you're gonna do what you wanna do about it, but my two cents is that you leave it alone. Just let everybody ride their own waves and come to their own destination. They're not married yet, so let them be and move on. You know what I always say; every dog has his day."

"True, and that's the same advice I would give you. It's just how I feel about her nagging at my heart. This information could be a game-changer if that dog's day was today." I wanted her back, and Mario knew it.

"It could change everything in a negative way too. On the upside, she might leave him. The downside is they grow even closer, and she pulls away from you for causing her pain by telling her. The messenger almost always gets shot. With your kids in her custody, you don't need that. Think about all of it, and I'm with you, whichever way you roll," Mario said before adding in a Chris Tucker voice, "**Damn,** this situation is messed up."

"Now you got Friday jokes? That's how you do me?"

"Nah, we good. Stay up, Mont."

"Thanks, bro. Talk to you later."

I hung up the phone with my thoughts no clearer than when I called my boy. I still had my finger hovering over Destiny's name on my phone, ready to expose Jacob's secret. She was always mine. Why should I give up at a time when I had such explosive ammo at my disposal?

Montie
Justine, Justine

The following week, I was still upset about finding out Tracye was a fake name Justine had given to get close to me. The past few days had been an emotional rollercoaster, tragic at worst. Justine, the woman that tried taking Destiny away from me, away from my children, had the last laugh. The last thing I wanted to do was have sex with that evil bitch. Rearrange her face, maybe, but not betray Destiny in that way, no matter how our relationship had turned out.

"Mr. Brown, you have a call on line two," Shalonda buzzed into my office. Thankful for the interruption from my thoughts, I answered immediately.

"Montie Brown speaking."

"Montie! I'm glad you answered," Justine's voice sang out.

"Make this the last time that you call me." I seethed.

"Oh, so now you want to act like we didn't share something beautiful this weekend?" she sounded bewildered.

"Why are you calling my place of business? I didn't share anything beautiful with you. I had a roll in the sack with a woman who called herself Tracye," I snapped out in a loud grate.

"I want to talk to you."

"We did all the talking we're going to do when I was in Miami. I'm done with you, so don't call me anymore and you had better not do anything to hurt Destiny." I felt the need to tell her that hurting Destiny was off-limits. "If you think you've ever felt wrath, times that by ten and imagine it happening to you repeatedly, if anything happens to the mother of my children," I warned with the unmitigated truth.

"Temper, temper." She laughed as if I'd told a hilarious joke. "I wish I was nearby. Angry sex is to die for."

"You can think I'm joking, but you haven't seen anything, Justine. Try me."

"Everyone thinks Destiny is worth protecting as if she is *so* precious. What about me? What about you and Jacob having me in your beds and taking all you wanted from me? I bet you didn't tell your precious Destiny that Jacob slept with me in their new house. Hell, I bet you didn't even tell her about us."

"That's no one's business but the people involved. Besides, who's to say you're not just lying about Jacob?"

"I don't tell lies."

"Well, who is *Tracye?*" I pulled the phone away from my ear, about to hang up on this mockery of a conversation.

66

"That part was a lie," she admitted. "I couldn't very well walk up to you and introduce myself as the woman everyone thinks is the devil's spawn, could I? You never would have given me a chance if you knew I was the same woman that..." she paused.

I finished her thought. "Put my ex-wife in the hospital? You're damn right; I wouldn't have. A chance to do what exactly? Ruin us even more? No, thank you," I argued.

"Montie, I'm sorry."

"Save your apology for someone who wants it. It's not like you wanted me; you just wanted to get close to Jacob and to humiliate Destiny."

"So maybe I did," she said, her voice growing sinister. "Who do you think you're kidding? I saw the way you looked at her at the rehearsal. You want her back. You want her so bad your soul is tortured by it. I've given you all the ammo you need to get what your heart desires. If she finds out that I slept with Jacob, she will come running back to your open arms. My plan will work."

"If you want your secret out, tell her yourself, Justine. Leave me out of it!" I barked.

"She won't believe me."

"Not my problem."

"But she'll listen to you, Montie."

"Again, not my problem. Now, if you would be so kind as to forget you met me, I would appreciate it," I said through clenched teeth. I could hear her pleading for me not to hang up on her as my phone dropped back down onto the receiver.

The drama had me reeling. I only had solace behind my desk, buried in paperwork and working hard to tune out the noise of my personal life. Justine's call threatened to break into that little bit of peace before I remembered the power of hanging up.

I vowed from that moment forward to put space between me and anything stressing me out, starting with Justine. Separating from Destiny would be more challenging, but I would take Mario's advice and stay out of it. It would be hard, considering my children bind me to her. I would have to look in her face knowing everything she was building was a lie.

The tiny, adorable faces of Montie Jr. and Montana assailed my mind. I let out a loud sigh as separation anxiety rushed all over me. Everything other than my love for my children was wrong, just wrong. My only two loves were miles away, being fathered by a cheater.

My phone rang again, pulling me out of my morbid thoughts.

"Montie, Holistic Medical is on your second line. It's the CEO," Shalonda's voice rang out over the intercom.

"Thank you," I said, pressing the button for my line and answering a call I welcomed. "Montie Brown speaking."

"Hello Montie, Mr. Bromage here. I'm calling to see how things are going with my software. My new computers came in today and have been installed. Once your tech people get your piece hooked up, I can have my office manager set up start dates for our admin people. We're eager to open for business and want to get some sort of a timeline."

"I understand your urgency, Mr. Bromage. I have a meeting tomorrow morning with a partner company I've contracted to help meet your deadline. I'll be able to give you a better estimate of go-live time after that meeting, for sure," I said.

"We need it within the next week, sooner if you can get it done this week," he coaxed as if coding software specific to his company's culture and guidelines was something he could pull up to the drive-thru window and order.

"Hey, I understand your readiness to get your hands on the software, but, like we discussed last week, when you signed your contract, it will take at least two weeks to get a test environment ready to review. It will be another week after that is approved for us to work out any kinks. That's provided those revisions are minimal."

"I can't wait three weeks to start," he barked an octave higher than before.

I wasn't surprised by Mr. Bromage rushing me. My customers thought I was a magic maker, and I delivered on that reputation for the most part. The last business working on his project didn't complete it in a timely fashion. He'd only called me last week with this difficult, detailed software order he wanted created from ground zero. Therefore, I had zero chill with being rushed.

"Mr. Bromage, I work as hard and fast as possible for all of my clients. That's my company's promise. My portfolio is filled with software deals that, as you know, were not thrown together. For perfection, you will have to give us time—at least a month total," I said.

He let out an irritated sigh and murmured something under his breath. I wasn't concerned about his impatience. Our contract stated everything, and I had a team of lawyers on standby for situations like this.

"Well, work as fast as you can," he said demandingly.

"Rest assured that you're in the best hands you'll be able to find in this area, if not the entire industry." *And that was a fact.*

"I'll follow up tomorrow," he said, hanging up the phone before I had the chance to let him know that calling every day would not speed up the process.

I dialed Shalonda's extension.

"Yes, sir."

"When Mr. Bromage calls from now on, take a message. I'll return his calls when I have time, okay?"

"Okay." Her voice was so soft that I knew she was grinning. I rarely put a client on my no-talk list, but I couldn't let Mr. Bromage worry me for two weeks. I was doing everything in my power to get his work done in half the time as it was.

"Is my meeting still set with Lissa McDaniels from Naytek tomorrow?" I asked Shalonda.

"Yes, sir, she will be here at 10 a.m."

"Good," I hung up and sat back in my chair.

I pulled up Lissa's website once again. Naytek had an impressive client list, including Emory University and the University of Alabama at Birmingham. Their medical coding designs were sleek, and the administration touted how user-friendly they were. I picked up my phone and called Lissa personally to see if there was anything I could do ahead of our meeting to make it more productive.

"Hello," a melodic voice answered on the second ring.

"Hi, is this Mrs. McDaniels?"

"This is she," she sounded warm and happy. I wondered if she always was that chipper.

"This is Montie Brown of True Colors Technology. We have a meeting tomorrow."

"Hi Mr. Brown, yes, I'm looking forward to our meeting! It's at ten, right?"

I smiled at the sound of her delicately sweet voice. It was a far cry from Justine's tone that had just grated my last nerve.

"Yes, it's at ten. And I'm looking forward to it too. We have a lot to get hashed out. I'm calling to see if there is anything specific you need from me ahead of tomorrow's meeting that would help me be more prepared for you?" I asked.

"Wow, it's rare that anyone calls to see what I need beforehand. I appreciate you doing that; however, I can't think of anything now. Shalonda was a huge help when I called for more information about the software you need to be designed. She has given me the specifics already."

Shalonda was worth her weight in gold. She took great notes at my client's meetings, was knowledgeable in coding and software design, and could easily stand in for me if I were unavailable.

"That's good to hear. Well, I'm excited about our meeting. Mr. Bromage at Holistic Medical is eager to get the final product in his hands. In fact, he called me today about it," I said.

"I'm confident that we can come up with something that he'll be satisfied with, so I'll see you tomorrow at ten?" she confirmed.

"See you then." I hung up the phone with a subconscious smile.

Lissa McDaniel's confidence left me feeling accomplished after chasing her down to secure a meeting with her. I couldn't wait to dive back into work with the best creatives in Atlanta.

Lissa

Yes, to Me

I laid down on the bed and picked up my book, *Year of Yes*, by Shonda Rhimes. It had been a while since I read a good book, especially one that didn't have to do with coding or selling software. If I wasn't reading those books, I was studying a new client's website to know the best way to secure a deal as the CEO of the fasting growing software design company in the south, Naytek Corp.

A friend referred Shonda's book to me when I was going through some drama with my last relationship. Boy, was I glad I took her advice and allowed this book to pour into me. Right off the bat, I enjoyed the quirky sense of humor and inspiration in telling the writer's life story. I reached the part where she said she would 'say Yes to saying No to people who were toxic in her life.'

I paused and just laid there, reflecting on the toxic people I'd said Yes to in my recent past. "What a way to put things into perspective," I said to my empty room. "I've been saying yes to all the wrong people."

First, there was Seth Baker, Mr. Smooth as a Chocolate Mimosa sitting on chill on a scorching hot summer day. I met him on a business trip, and by the night's end, I was singing his name to everyone on our floor at the Hilton. At the end of the business conference, we both went our separate ways but stayed in touch. We had frequent bump and grind hookups that caused me to fall in love with him.

I invited Seth completely into my world. A gesture he didn't return. He kept me out in the cold, not letting me know much about him besides his body and where he worked. Seth led me on, pretended to want to be with me more than I craved cheesecake. When I was so deep into his love that I couldn't stand to breathe without him around, that was when I found out about his wife and kids.

Next up was Jameson Brown. I just knew Jameson would be different from Seth. He was a single lawyer, a preacher's son, and had a milk chocolate physique that just melted in your mouth. We started with a slow, simmering heat, building our friendship before an explosive fire detonated among us. I thought that set him apart from Seth. I let my guard down until Rhonda, a woman from his past, resurfaced, ready to resume their puppy love from grade school.

I felt hurt by Jameson dumping me for Rhonda, but I also felt sorry for him. Rhonda was obsessed with my best friend's life so much that she stole Shayla's husband's sperm, implanted it into herself, and had his child. I thought that bit of news would have been enough to shake some sense into Jameson. However, he stood by her side until she was locked away in a mental institution. Knowing him, he's probably petitioning the courts to get her an early release. Jameson had only used me as a filler until his bat shit crazy high school sweetheart returned. Then he ran away just as fast as Seth did.

My last two attempts at love taught me a lot about wasting time. I made myself available to men too quickly. All they had to do was be fine and sexy, and I was there for their every beckoning call. I had to be more careful about reading a person's true intentions. Everyone that smiled and appeared to enjoy my company wasn't into me the same way I was into them. Hard lessons had been learned about what was fair in the game of love.

Lying there with nothing to show for my affection—not a plaque, a t-shirt, not even a thank you for the good time, I knew I needed to turn my way of thinking around. How many times had I worked tirelessly to satisfy a man only to find myself in this place of nothingness?

This would be my year of Yes to myself and No to others.

"I needed to read this book. This is good," I said as I turned the page.

I finished off the current chapter and laid my book on the empty space of the bed beside me. Exhaustion lulled me into a light slumber with a feeling of liberation from the positive thoughts that had swirled through my mind.

The next morning, I woke up and sat up in bed, yawning. I stretched my arms wide, and a smile followed suit as my hand came down on the book beside me. I beamed at the gentle reminder that today was the beginning of my own year of saying Yes to myself and No to others' needs. I got my rejuvenated butt out of bed and headed to the bathroom.

After dressing in a cute blue dress with an oversized navy-blue belt and matching blue shoes, I spun in the mirror. I was headed to see my new client, Mr. Brown, at True Colors Technology Group. I looked damn good. I was confident I'd be able to sell Montie one of our consultant packages.

Lord, as a side note, I hope he's no relation to Jameson Brown. I don't even want to be in the presence of Jameson's family. So far, my research hasn't shown any relation.

I stopped in the kitchen and popped a bagel in the toaster. I grabbed a bottle of orange juice and the bagel and headed out the door.

GPS brought me to a shopping center with a large department store, grocery store, and other businesses like nail shops and restaurants. A huge colorful sign caught my attention at the end of the company row. It had all the rainbow colors with fluorescent lights displaying the different colors.

You are a badass, Lissa. You crush business deals for breakfast and spit them out by lunch. I internally chanted the mantra I had been repeating since I threw myself into work after Jameson left me feeling lost.

When I woke up from that train wreck of a relationship, I returned stronger with my career as my new love. Knowing that

76

I could bring millions of dollars of revenue to my company annually by the work of my own hands became my midnight embrace.

After reapplying lipstick to my puckered lips, I fixed my face and stepped out into the cool morning air. I was glad the Atlanta sun wasn't beaming down yet. In April, it could go either way. One year, we would be subject to snow in the spring, and the following year be a victim of the smoldering sun.

I walked into a clean, modernly decorated lobby and was greeted by a receptionist sitting behind an oversized marble desk.

"Hello, my name is Shalonda. How may I help you?" she asked in an upbeat tone.

"Hi, Shalonda. We've been chatting on the phone. I'm Lissa Daniels. Here for my appointment with Mr. Montie Brown," I said, holding a folder firmly under my arm as I extended my hand to shake hers.

"Yes, we have! Nice to meet you. Mr. Brown is expecting you," the woman rose to her feet, revealing her tall stature. She shook my hand. "Please follow me."

I followed the gorgeous, slender waist and thick everywhere else woman down a short, glossy blue hallway with vibrant splashes of color on the walls. The hall led to an office with a plaque on the door that read Montie Brown.

Shalonda knocked on the door and entered after hearing a smooth voice say, "Come in."

When I entered the room, uniquely decorated like the rest of the building, I noticed a prominent, medium brown-skinned man unfolding from his seat. My eyes blinked carefully to clear my vision for the site before me. Montie Brown flashed a mouthful of pearly whites and whatever I had cleared went blurry.

Oh, trouble loomed, and I could feel it all over. This man could get it if I wasn't starting my Year of No to Yes, or was it Yes to No?

"Thanks for showing Ms. McDaniels in, Shalonda," his velvety voice ignited a flame in me as he nodded at his receptionist.

Shalonda returned the gesture and left out, closing the door behind her.

With all the rainbow colors on his logo and splashed over his walls, I just imagined he would be a little more, I don't know...

He's probably undercover anyway. That's what I told myself to ward off any lustful feelings from surfacing. However, when he spoke so smooth yet powerful, I was immediately swept up in his sweet, honey, molasses tone.

"How are you this morning, Ms. McDaniels?" he asked, extending noticeably lickable fingers in my direction.

Oh shit. Time for a pep talk. Lissa McDaniels, if you don't get your act together, I internally scolded like my best friend, Shayla, would if she were in the room. The ready-to-play naughty girl that lived dormant inside me needed a swift kick in the backside.

I internally chided myself back to some sense of sanity.

Year of Yes to No.

Year of yes to no.

Year of...

"Lissa, you can call me Lissa." I finally extended my hand to shake his.

"Please, have a seat. I'm glad you could make the meeting on such short notice," he said, cordial and all business. Following his lead would keep me out of the fantasy I kept drifting off into and into the business at hand.

"When a company like yours calls, we listen. So glad to be able to meet with you to talk about the great things Naytek will be able to do for you."

"Well, let's get started then," he said with a smile.

"I understand you are looking for the right software to include a coding and billing module and a medical transcription and archives link. You want it colorful and easy for the end-user to maneuver. Plus, you want something unique to the holistic industry."

Mr. Brown's eyes roamed over my face. He appeared impressed that I understood the product he intended to create. "Yes, that's exactly what I need, Lissa."

"Since we specialize in the medical transcription and archives piece, we'll work closely with you to incorporate the coding and billing modules so your customer will be happy. We can add some funky fonts and color schemes into our final coding, and I'm sure they will also be happy with the high technological side. The most important thing is to make sure it's functional and cutting edge," I said.

"Yes, the look is important, but it should be highly functional and better than anything else on the market," he sat back in his seat, his eyes roaming over my face as if he were thinking about something that was not apparent.

I slid the white paper I had prepared specifically for him and waited for him to thumb through it. Yet, he still sat there and stared at me. "I think you'll find sufficient information in this documentation." I extended the papers to him.

He took them and skimmed through the papers. "Whoa, I've never had anyone come into my office for a meeting, and in the first five minutes, I already have everything I need. This is damn impressive."

"Thank you, Mr. Brown, I—"

"You can call me Montie. I feel we're going to need to know each other on a first-name basis," he conveyed, still browsing through the white paper.

"Excuse me?"

"Yes, call me Montie. You asked me to call you Lissa, right? We're about the same age, so you have no reason to call me by my surname. I want you to call me Montie."

"Okay, Montie." I giggled when I said his name. For no reason, I fucking giggled.

He chuckled over my odd amusement of simply saying his name.

"So, when do we sign the contracts?" I eased back into business mode. I didn't get where I was by flattering sexy men.

"I'm seriously ready after seeing how prepared you are. You have remarkable references, and everything you laid out here shows an in-depth understanding of my company and the client I asked you to build the software for. I value providing our clients with vibrant and colorful applications, and I believe you can carry out the tasks we need down to the letter."

"I'm glad you can see the value in what I do."

He gave me an intense look. "I definitely do."

"Thank you." I smiled. "I'll bring over a mockup disk for you to see if we're headed in the right direction. If it meets your satisfaction, we can sign the contract and complete the project within a week or two."

"That works well for me. If it's a go, I'd like to work closely with you until it's complete. This is worth millions to me because this clinic is a part of a huge network of holistic clinics popping up around the country. The national director of computer systems is looking for something better than what they currently have, and they chose us, which is a big deal."

"Wow, that *is* a big deal."

He nodded and continued. "They'll try this out on a new clinic, but this could be tapped for the entire network and could end up bringing in a couple hundred thousand for you."

"That sounds very doable."

"It has to be perfect, though. If we can develop unique software and farm it out to hospitals and medical clinics nationwide, we'll license it and see revenue for years."

"Say no more…." I said, liking the feeling of making a deal with a go-getter who I was sure would soon be a satisfied customer.

For the next hour, we discussed details, down to the things we thought were eye-catching, unique, and user-friendly. When we finished, I had enough information to take back to my implementation team for a bang-up software creation.

I felt extremely successful as I walked to my car. Not because of the impending business deal, but because I looked into the honey-brown eyes of the sexiest chocolate man alive and resisted the urge to sleep with him. I allowed the new me to enter the room and smash a business deal without anything extra taking place.

As much as I wanted to flirt with him, I didn't. I successfully said No to the possibility of another failed relationship and Yes to my future in business. I chuckled at my small win.

Reading good books matter.

Montie
A Shift in Me

I stared at the chair she'd sat in long after she left. A cosmic glow still illuminated the space she occupied. Those thick, brown sugar thighs crossed and uncrossed seamlessly as she pushed her glasses back on her nose and talked about intricate details, industry standards, and software encryption. The navy dress she wore had fought gallantly to cover all the goodness God saw fit to bestow upon her thick legs, but the brave material failed miserably. Her voluptuous beauty burst through the seams of the fabric, leaving me to ruminate over every inch of buried sweetness that couldn't find the light of day.

Visions of Destiny cut into my thoughts. Lissa was about the same height and stature; her soft and velvety voice reminded me of the only woman to hold my heart. Not the Destiny that's Jacob's fiancée, but the young girl I met and fell in love with back in college. The one I worked my ass off for, so I could give her the world. The same woman who thought that hard work was a threat to my love for her. The same one that Jacob Turner's probably plying into right now to express his deceitful love. That thought alone threatened to make the woman whose essence hung in the room like a painting less palatable.

Lissa had been unaware of my time travel as she sat before me, sharing her endless intellect. She also appeared unaware of how much her presence had affected me, taking me back to a time when my life had no drama and I knew love in its purest form.

Lissa didn't need to know that I was drawn to her because she reminded me so much of my ex-wife or that I had to adjust my slacks as the thought of pulling her up unto my desk and becoming one flesh with hers came to mind. Thankfully, she didn't notice my burning desire to take her into my arms and own her like she was mine, if only for a short while.

Memories of the last woman I plowed into oblivion while trying to release myself from the hold Destiny had on me flooded my mind. The Tracye, a.k.a. Justine fling, had ended in disaster, and her name alone was an anti-erection.

I shook away my conflicted thoughts and snapped back into my workday. Thinking of Justine did the trick. The last thing I needed was another distraction. I had a tremendous workload, and clients were crawling up my ass.

I picked up Lissa's contract and inattentively scanned the document. "She's a beast in the way she handles her business. She's probably a beast at everything she does." My tongue slid across the length of my lips, thinking about how beastly she could be in bed. "She's probably hard to satisfy, too," I added to ward off any thoughts of crossing the line we'd just established as business partners. I had no plan to revisit love and end up with a woman who, no matter what I did, didn't see that it was all for her.

Love would have to wait for me, probably forever. More importantly, I had to figure out how to stay relevant in my children's lives so many miles away, and I had to complete Mr. Bromage's software in a week. Everything else, including whatever sparks I felt flow between Lissa and me, I didn't have time for.

I pushed back from my desk, stood, and walked to the front of my office building.

"Montie, did your meeting go well with Ms. McDaniels?" Shalonda asked when I stood in front of her desk.

"It did. Working with Lissa is going to help a lot. She's really impressive."

"Uh-huh." Shalonda sat for a second staring at me. "Well, we know she's qualified because we checked her out. You wouldn't have had her here if she wasn't the best."

"Yeah." I paused and looked at Shalonda. "Why are you looking at me like that, though?"

"Like what?" she asked.

"Like that," I said, causing her to gaze back at her computer screen.

"Oh, I was just agreeing with you, boss man," she said as she tapped away on her keyboard.

"Sure." I patted my pockets to feel for my car keys and took them out.

Shalonda murmured, "But she does look a lot like Destiny."

"You noticed that, too," I asked.

"Yeah, it was surreal when she came through the lobby and introduced herself," she said.

"I thought I was the only one that picked up on that." I changed the subject. "I have to make a few runs. I'll be back in about an hour, maybe two."

"Got you covered, boss," I heard Shalonda say behind me as I walked out into the midday sun.

Unlike that chilly morning, the sun's mean glare was proof that spring quickly faded into summer. The heat immediately reminded me that I had donned a full Brook Brother's suit that morning. I slid off my jacket and held it until I got into the car. I drove straight to the gym.

I slept so terribly last night I didn't feel like going when I woke up, but I needed to get some good energy working inside my body before finishing my day. It seemed like everything that could happen had happened to me in the past year. The gym had become my only source of energy to pull through.

When I pulled up, I was glad to see that the parking lot wasn't full. Tuesdays weren't usually that busy and not in the middle of the day. I grabbed my gym bag from the trunk and strolled in. "Hey, Mario. What's up, man?" I dapped up my friend and trainer. He had sweat running down the front of his

T-shirt, so I knew he was getting it in already. We ended our handshake with a snap.

"Man, just in here putting some work on these young boys. It's good seeing you, Mont. I wasn't expecting you since you ain't been in in a while. You slacking today, or are you ready to sweat blood?"

"I know I haven't been in a while, but I have a lot of built-up tension that I need to work off, so let's get to it," I said, adding, "I need to relieve some stress."

"Did something new go down?" Mario asked.

"I don't even want to talk about it."

"Something else since last night?" he pressed.

"Yeah, the ol' girl called me this morning playing games."

"Who, Justine?"

"Yeah, man. You already know."

"What did she want?"

"For me to tell Destiny about her and Jacob." I shook my head. "But I'm not getting in the middle of that. I'm only concerned about my kids being in another state. I've been trying to be the bigger man, but it's been working on me since I took them to Miami."

"What you did for Destiny during your marriage and your divorce is more than most men would have the balls to do. Going to the rehearsal dinner to see them practice for the wedding is more than I could handle." Mario offered me a sincere look. "Don't beat yourself up about the way things ended up. You did your best," he added.

"I'm not beating myself up. I'm just getting used to having to visit my kids in another state. What if there's an emergency?"

"Are you sure that's all you're worried about?"

"That's the only thing that's bothering me."

"First thing you must do is be honest with yourself, man. It'll help you move past it much quicker. I'm telling you. I've been there."

"I *am* honest with myself," I growled.

"But last night, you said—"

"Damn, man, I should've never talked to you about this if all you were going to do was throw shit I told you up in my face. Besides, what do you know about love when you're always chasing the next big booty? You ain't ever been in a committed relationship, as far back as I can remember. Now, you have all this advice for me."

"I know more than you think," Mario said defensively. "And you're the one that's always asking my advice, so I was just giving it."

"Look, man, I might as well go run the block or something. It's obvious I won't be able to relieve any stress in here," I said, looking around at the people who were at ease pumping iron and on the cardio machines.

Mario threw his hands up in the air in surrender. "I was just trying to look out for you, bro. I didn't mean any harm at all. But since you're throwing shots and can't take them back, I know you need your space right now. I need to get back to these youngstas anyway. Look at them." He tilted his head toward the weights. A scrawny kid standing over the weight bench that was supposed to be spotting a slightly overweight guy could barely pick the bar up off the other dude's chest. "I'm thirty-two years old, and I pump that steel better than him. They don't have nothing on me. How do these lil youngstas, who used to be football stars in college, come in here and can't lift two twenty?" Mario successfully changed the subject to something lighter.

"That's ridiculous. You better get over there and spot them before they both end up in the ER," I laughed, glad to finally release good energy with my friend and trainer.

"Nah, they'll be fine," Mario said as the spotter mustered enough strength to put the bar back on the bench.

"You're right, Mario."

Mario laughed. "I knew he could do it."

"No, I mean, you're right about how I feel about Destiny. I'm still in love with her. I'm still fuming that she moved on so fast. I thought I wasn't, but seeing them together, in their home, the life they're building...it was more than any ex should have to sit through. I hate I didn't get a chance to claim what was mine before another man did—a man I now know doesn't deserve her."

"You didn't do anything wrong, Montie. I want you to keep telling yourself that."

"I kept waiting for my business to hit this mark and that mark, and never once did I stop and go after what was really important to me. In that sense, I failed."

"So, what? Now you know what not to do the next time you find the right one."

"I told you there will be no other right one. She was it, Mario. There will be no second time around for me. I'm done with even trying. From now on, it's smash and dash for me." I pumped my arm slowly, motioning how I planned to hit it and quit it from that day forward. "That's just how it has to be."

"You're just saying that mess right now. I'm telling you, the right one hasn't come along yet. When she does, she'll have your ass pussy whipped and pining over her too. You won't even be able to think about Destiny because you'll be wrapped around her finger. And because I know you have good judgment and have learned from your past mistakes, she will be a good woman who feels the same way about you."

I shook my head. "Nah, no second love for me. She ain't coming. If she does, I'm not cuffing her. Trust that." We both laughed at my choice of words.

"You say that now, but when you see her, she will leave you wondering if Destiny was ever worth the trouble, Mont. I'm telling you."

"Bruh, you ain't no Dr. Phil," I pretended to throw a blow at him and walked toward the dressing room. Mario was a player, so there was no way he knew when or if I'd ever find love. He hadn't even found it for himself. I turned to face him when I got close to the locker room. "I didn't come to whine about women. I came to pump this iron. We gon' do this or not?"

Mario flexed his chest muscles. "I stay ready. Get yourself changed, and we'll start your warm-ups."

"That's what I'm talking about." I was ready to work out blood, sweat, and tears.

*****

After a grueling training session, I felt one hundred percent better. I meandered into the dressing room, showered, and dressed in my suit and tie, minus the jacket. My mind felt relaxed, and I was ready to return to the office and superman the day.

"Good workout, man," Mario said as I passed him to leave. He stood close to the front counter, greeting guests as they came and went.

"Thought you were trying to kill a brother on those squats, but at least my head is much clearer. I feel a million times better."

"That's what it's all about," he shot back. The anxious look on his face grew by the second.

I knew his reply would be something I didn't want to hear. Yet, I asked, "What's wrong with you?"

"I want to say one more thing about what we talked about when you came in."

"Bruh," I sighed exasperatedly. "I thought you were in the business of selling your services for positive endorphins. Didn't I just tell you that I feel better? Are you trying to stress me the hell out again?"

"No, I don't want to do that. I just want to leave you with something to think about."

Thinking was exactly the thing I was trying to escape. I slid my arm into my jacket. Since he was intent on dragging me back down, I might as well have taken the time to do something constructive. I didn't want to hear about me moving on and finding another woman. That was the furthest thing from my mind. As far as I was concerned, after the Justine trick, I would be on a hands-only diet for a while where women were involved.

"Spill it, Mario. I have to get back to work," I barked. He was taking too long to respond.

"Just don't close your eyes to what's around you," he finally blurted.

"What is that supposed to mean?"

"The real one could be right in front of your face. It could be someone God has already sent your way, and you overlooked her because you still want to see Destiny by your side. Hell, it could be your fine-ass secretary, for all you know. Crawl out of Destiny's ass for a minute and think about that hot piece of—"

"Who Shalonda?" I shook my head profusely. "Nah, man. That's strictly professional."

His brow rose in interest. "So, you're saying you never even thought about tapping that?"

"Yeah, that's what I'm saying. Strictly professional."

"Good for me, then," Mario rubbed his hands together. "If you don't holler at her, I'm going for it."

"You have a thing for Shalonda?"

"Man, that lady is slim in the right places and super thick in all the right places. I would've tapped that by now. I thought you had her—"

"I don't look at her that way," I cut him off. "She's the one that keeps me together businesswise, and I want it to stay that way. Sex complicates shit, as you can see."

"Well, I'm taking applications for new complications," Mario laughed.

"Aight, man, I'm 'bout to get out of here," I said and extended my hand to give him some dap.

"Alright, man, stay up," Mario encouraged, pulling me in for a brotherly hug. "Just keep your eyes open. Your blessing could be staring you in the face. That's all I'm saying. I can't say I'm sad that you haven't blessed yourself with Shalonda, though." He bit down on his lips. "Mmph, mmph, mmph. I'm going to have fun with her."

I blinked my eyes to prevent sexual thoughts of Shalonda from entering my mind. "Holler at you later, man," I said and walked out the door.

Montie
Her

I smelled her before I saw her. I paused in the foyer to partake of the delightful scent wafting through the air a while longer before I walked into the reception area of True Colors.

Lissa waited beside Shalonda's desk. As I stared at her, I couldn't help but think about what Mario said about my blessing staring me in the face. Did Lissa possess the power to make me forget about Destiny? The mere fact that the question lingered in the air validated that thought.

No. I damned the renegade musings from wandering aimlessly around my tortured mind, and my attention went to a flowing bouquet of flowers sitting on the counter in front of Lissa.

"Nice flowers, Shalonda," I said, including Lissa and Shalonda in my gaze. As far as I knew, Shalonda didn't have a special guy to send her flowers.

"I think it's sweet that you have someone special to send you flowers, Montie," Lissa spoke up and winked at me. "Shalonda and I were just admiring how pretty the bouquet is...I remember those days." Lissa's gaze left mine and fell to the briefcase in her hand.

"These aren't yours?" I asked as my questioning gaze moved to Shalonda.

"No, they're yours, boss."

I looked at Lissa. She raised her hands innocently, dousing the idea that the beautiful woman had hand-delivered me flowers. "I didn't bring them here," she confirmed.

"I don't know what I was thinking," I tried to recover.

"There's a card attached. Would you like me to read it for you?" Shalonda asked, taking the card off the bunch.

"No, thank you. I'll take it from here," I removed the card from her hand and left the bouquet on the front desk.

I strolled to my office with Lissa on my trail. The click of her heels behind me sent images through my mind of her bountiful ass that I knew was bouncing along with her poised stride. "Sorry, I wasn't set up when you arrived," I said.

"It's really not a problem. I got here a little early."

"Now that I know you are an early bird, I'll never just be on time again. I'll come early." I smiled, hoping to lighten the mood and see her pretty smile in return.

The best part about working with Lissa would be the brightness she brought into the room. Her cheeks turned up, delighting me with her shimmering beauty as she took her seat on the opposite side of my desk.

95

"I just wanted to make sure you weren't waiting on me. That's all," she said coyly.

She sucked me into her air with that smile like she did yesterday. Her essence overpowered the room, extracting my greatest loss from the atmosphere and implanting her winning spirit wherever there was once despair. All my problems faded away, and I only saw Lissa McDaniels. Either she was a damn good businesswoman with the knack to reset the atmosphere to achieve her intended effect, or she was a real live angel sent to show me the light of the new day. Just like Mario said would happen.

I gripped my hand tight as if that would help me get a grasp on my wandering thoughts. The firmness of the card from the flowers cradled my palm. I looked down at the envelope and glanced inside to see who had sent the arrangement. Seeing Destiny's name compelled me to read the entire card.

Montie,

I didn't get a chance to tell you goodbye face to face before you left Miami, but I take from your abrupt departure and not attending the wedding that you just weren't ready for all of this. I'll give you time to come around, and I know you will. I just want to tell you again how much I thank you for being such a great man and father. I will always love you as a true friend should –
Destiny.

I held the card as my eyes roamed over the words I had just read. It wasn't in her handwriting but signed with her name.

I dropped the card down onto the papers in front of me on my desk.

"Wow! Must be someone really special," Lissa's voice scissored into my thoughts.

"Why do you say that?" I asked nonchalantly, pushing the papers in front of me aside.

"The look on your face when you read that card. I don't know. You just seemed to be taken to another place, another time," Lissa stopped short of saying more.

I shoved the card off my desk and into a top drawer. "Yeah, it's the mother of my kids thanking me for co-parenting with her while she lives in Florida. She moved there to be with her new husband."

"That's impressive, Montie. Co-parenting, that is."

I looked intently into her eyes. She was only attempting to be supportive in her small talk. However, I had no interest in hearing how great I'd been by allowing my children to move states over without protest. I should have fought harder for my kids to stay in Atlanta. I should have fought harder for my marriage.

As if sensing the inappropriateness of getting into my personal business, Lissa slid a CD across the desk to me. "I was up all night sketching this out and had one of my best developers come at four this morning to finish the preliminary draft. Of course, remember that the final quality will be much better, but I think you will appreciate our headwork."

"Let's see what you have," I took the CD from her hand and popped it into my computer.

"It will work better on their computers set up for the test environment, but you can definitely try it on your computer."

97

"I have this computer souped up with all of the latest software and hardware," I assured her as a colorful display with Mr. Bromage's company logo popped up on my screen. A clean-looking application with an exquisite array of fonts was on the next screen. I was impressed with the quality of her mock-up.

"What do you think?" she asked, anxious to hear my thoughts.

"It looks...damn good," I scrolled through a few screens. "And it's user-friendly with all the modules highly visible at the top."

"I wrote it to work best with Mr. Bromage's computers."

"This is the direction we want to go in," I said calmly while wondering where she'd been all my life. There's nothing like a motivated, well-spoken woman and a freaking genius. She was exactly the type of smart person I needed on my team. "Where have you been all my life?" I asked with a hearty smile spread easily across my face.

Lissa's cute smile teased the corners of her lips. "I've been waiting for you to consult my firm."

"Well, now that we're together. Imagine the things we will do."

"We don't have to imagine. Let's just take over the world."

"Deal," I reached inside my desk, pulled out her contract, and signed it. "Sign on the dotted line, and I'll get Shalonda to make us each a copy," I told her. Once the formalities were out of the way, we dug deeper into the software.

"So, you want the quick close feature removed and the sign-out prompts added?" she asked thirty minutes later.

"Yes, that'll decrease the chance of making a billing error when they get kicked out. Now, they can stop and work on something else and still not lose what they were working on. That's one of the things the billing department will need."

"We don't want any errors. It should be a foolproof system by the time we're done." She paused to think. "I'll tell you what. I'll get these updates back to you in the morning, and you can work on any improvements on your end after that. If you can return the corrections tomorrow evening or the next day, I think we can have something finalized within four days. My other projects with a later due date have been put on hold, and this is our main objective."

"That sounds lovely. If this is done by Friday and I can get my tech writers to draw up a user guideline by Monday, we will look it over, test it out Monday, and present it to the client on Tuesday."

She nodded confidently. "I like that timeline. It's stringent, but what's a challenge to a couple of giants?"

I looked into her determined brown eyes and smiled. "I love the way you think."

Lissa
No Fake Friends

"Hey, friend!" I said to Shayla in a high-pitched greeting when she waddled into my office that evening, carrying her eight-month pregnancy as though it pained her to the core. Shayla Davis and I became close friends when I rented out my office space in our building five years ago. Her psychiatry practice located downstairs made us the only two black women business owners in the plaza. We just clicked from day one.

"Hey, girl." She sat down and took a deep breath. "I can't wait until Glory brings her jumpy butt out with the rest of us," she rubbed her super pregnant belly. "She is giving me fits today."

I laughed. "Don't rush my shugga bear. She'll be here soon enough."

"Yeah, says the woman who still has her perfectly flat stomach and round booty that's not inflated by pregnancy hormones and cravings." Shayla shot me a deadly look. "Have I told you that you make me sick today?" she asked jokingly, then sat down and pretend pouted.

"I'm not falling for your stinky mood swings today. All I will say to you, my beautiful friend, is thank you for giving me two babies to love on without the responsibility of carrying and caring for them around the clock. You and your baby-making womb are a blessing to me." I giggled.

She rolled her eyes and blew out a gush of air. "What are you in such a good mood for?" Shayla asked as she finally settled into a comfortable spot in the chair. "And will you please invest in bigger chairs? I'm stuffed in this tiny seat like a dough girl. I'm sure your clients are uncomfortable, too. You need to get some chairs like I have in my office."

I waved her off. "Whatever, no one told you to grow a badonka donk. That has nothing to do with the chairs."

I could tell she didn't want to laugh, but she unwillingly let out the tiniest of a giggle. "It's Glory. She has me eating like a madwoman, and my pant size keeps growing. If I hit sixteen, I'm going through the roof."

"My god-baby has your fat cells by the collar," I teased. "I bet you'll stop and think about that the next time Antonio tries to jump your bones."

Shayla's husband, Antonio, couldn't keep his hands off her since they resolved their issues with Rhonda Wilson, the girl Jameson dumped me for. She was Shayla's ex-best friend that had an affair with Shayla's first husband and then tried and failed to seduce her second, Antonio. Since Rhonda couldn't get

Antonio to creep with her, she stole his sperm from the sperm bank and conceived his child without his consent. That woman was loopier than the whole ward of loonies in the state hospital.

"Oh, shut up," Shayla cut into my thoughts. "I didn't know I was already two months pregnant when we went through that drama with Rhonda. God forbid if I would have lost my baby dealing with her. My world would have crumbled down completely."

"Karma is making right what Rhonda was trying to make wrong for everyone," I paused. "Won't she do it?" I snapped my fingers to celebrate Karma, the dirty bitch.

"Yes, she did, and yes, she will," Shayla snapped her fingers and laughed.

"Since I have accomplished making you laugh, enough about Rhonda," I said.

Sadness entered Shayla's eyes as she thought about her friend. "Yeah, enough. That girl can put a damper on anyone's day. I just hope the judge doesn't let her out any time soon. After what she did, I don't want her to see the light of day for years. I truly don't think she needs to because she's always fixated on something delusional where I'm concerned."

"The only thing worse than a true hater is a fake friend. We both know she's so jealous of you that she doesn't know what to do with herself when she's not trying to steal what you have." Steam rose inside me at the thought of Rhonda bothering my friend again. "She'd better leave you alone if she knows what's good for her," I warned. I would go to war for my friend and put my range lessons to good use if Rhonda even imagined harming Shayla again.

"I just worry about it sometimes. Especially since I'm pregnant and can't really defend myself," Shayla admitted.

"She's locked up and not getting out any time soon. You don't have anything to worry about."

"That does very little to calm my nerves after everything we've been through. Anyway, did you skip lunch today?" Shayla asked, notably changing the course of the conversation. Her small hands rested above her rounded belly, letting me know the talk about Rhonda was causing her tension in her stomach.

"You didn't call me like you usually do, so I ended up working right through it," I admitted. "I thought you skipped lunch, too."

"Nah, I didn't skip it. I just brought something from home. I thought you might be busy since you've been out of the office this week in meetings. Maybe the reason you've not been in your office will be the answer to my original question."

"What question?" I asked, confused.

"What has you in such a good mood today?"

"I'm the same as I always am. Nothing new," I turned my see-through gaze back to my computer. I never had a poker face, so I was sure Shayla could see right through me.

"Oh, no. You sat there looking at your computer when I came in and cheesed like you just hit the Mega Millions. I would have thought young Denzel was about to step out of the screen, give you a lap dance, and then present you with your lottery check." She wore a conspiratorial expression on her face as she stared at me expectantly.

"Ha! You have a great imagination, Shayla."

"But I'm always right, so spread the joy with me. I need something to smile about too, as hot and miserable as I've been."

"Oh my," I bubbled with glee when Glory chose to run her foot across the expanse of Shayla's stomach.

"Ugh." She let out a sharp breath, froze still, and moaned until Glory was situated in her belly.

I sat back in my seat. "I was smiling when you came in, but it was nothing worth conversation. That's why Glory is warning you to leave me alone."

"Nothing worth conversation, huh?" Shayla repeated in a dry tone. "Come again, and remember that this is me you're talking to."

My meeting with Montie Brown merited conversation, verbal elation, and stimulation. It was hard to fight off temptation where Montie was concerned, but unfortunately, there was no news to share with my friend beyond our business relationship. I told her, "I just opened a pretty lucrative business deal. That's all."

She peered at me as if she already knew that an alluring, sexy man was on the other end of the transaction. "What kind of deal?" she asked and clung to every word that had yet to come out of my mouth.

"With the devil, honey." I stood and walked around to sit on the edge of my desk in front of an even more intrigued

Shayla. "He's this sexy as the devil man named Montie Brown, who's outsourcing one of his software projects to us."

Shayla's side-eye was strong as she studied me. "Well, you're the best he could have found for coding software."

"Yeah, my team will do a bang-up job working with him. He will be pleased." As much as I tried to fight away the thought of it, the inescapable vision of a satisfied look on Montie's face as he did a bang-up job on me impaled my brain.

"I have no doubt about that," Shayla said, calling my attention back to her side-eye.

"About what?" I asked, having gotten lost in my own banter.

"You'll do a good job for your client, and he will be pleased. Where is your head at? Wait a minute. You're smitten with him already. No, what am I saying? Of course, my dear friend, who falls in love at first sight, is smitten with him already. Come on, Lissa...no."

"Oh, Shayla. I can't stop thinking about doing things that have nothing to do with my assignment. I only have a track record of lasting a few weeks before I pounce on someone like him, so the struggle is about to get real having to be in the same space with the finger-licking good, recently divorced, and very eligible bachelor."

"Cry me a river." Shayla's fierce eyes cut a hole into me. "You can handle not jumping that man's bones if you exercise some self-control."

Self-control. That's exactly what I charged myself with doing this year. The 'year of yes to no.' It's incredibly amazing how fast that went out the window when Montie's chocolate brown orbs licked me up and down, and I didn't want him to stop. But hey, that was just sexual frustration—something I'd be damned if I let it get in the way of true happiness again.

Whew. Glad I had that talk with myself. Now back to Shayla.

"I'm trying to control myself, Shayla. A man like Montie Brown gets all in your pores, though," I began.

"Oh, where have I heard that line before?"

"I've never said that."

"Yes, you did. You said it about Seth when we were on the airplane headed home from that conference, and you also said, 'it is going to be hard to go back to Atlanta and not think about him.'"

"I was such a poor and misguided soul back then." I shook my head. "And you had no sympathy for my pain then, and you still have none now."

Shayla nodded. "You're right about that. I don't have sympathy for you. You decide whom to let in your life. When Titus was sleeping with Rhonda right under my nose, I decided to ignore it and pretend it would go away. I sacrificed my happiness for a sham marriage until I woke up and decided to face the music. If you jump in the sack with Montie, knowing that you have major business on the line and that he's likely an Atlanta bed hopper, that's you. I don't advise it, but I won't be mad at you either. I'll be here for you in the end, good or bad—matron of honor or cellmate."

"That's what I love about you. I get endless free hood therapy sessions."

She chuckled. "You're welcome."

I admitted, "I'm working hard to stay on the right track, and sometimes I need a nudge back to the other side." Having confided my thoughts about Montie to Shayla, I still hadn't convinced myself to never cross the line with him.

When Shayla left my office and I was alone again, I forbade the memories of Montie to enter my mind for the remainder of the day as my team and I worked diligently on the Holistic Medical software. I had to get used to work being my midnight passion. There was no prospect of any other love.

Montie
Hard Work

"Why if it isn't Mr. Montie Brown of True Colors Technology! I was beginning to think your true colors were dodging my phone calls," Mr. Bromage's sarcasm greeted me when I entered his office on a surprise visit.

Certain that the contents of my briefcase would make him a very happy man, I cracked a half-grin and planted a firm handshake on him.

"Mr. Bromage, I haven't been dodging your calls. I've been working. That's what software coders do; we work behind our computers and leave the phone conversations to our assistants," I corrected him in a tone that brooked no further bloviating.

"Well, I've been calling and leaving messages with your secretary. She said you were busy each time. I expect an open line of communication with all my service providers," Mr. Bromage said.

"Shalonda's able to answer any questions you may have in the future. She's as knowledgeable about your project and any questions that you may have as I am. If there's something she can't answer, she'll find the answer and get it to you within the hour." A few moments of dead silence lingered between us. "On a different note, I think you'll be more interested in what I was able to produce for you."

"Touché." Mr. Bromage pointed to the seat in front of his desk, then walked around and sat behind his.

"As you know, I promised your software in one month with a stretch goal of two weeks." I began unlatching my briefcase. "I'm pleased to present the final product to you today, ahead of schedule and under budget."

"You have it ready now?" he beamed with a huge smile spreading across his usually stoic face.

I nodded. "I have the beta software prepared."

"That's worth the wait and all the missed calls, Mr. Brown. When can we get it loaded on our computers," he squeaked out an octave higher than his usual voice.

"First, we need to test it out. Would you have time to do that if we set up a test environment on one of your PCs?"

"Are you kidding? I have nothing but time for this. Hold on." He picked up his phone and dialed a series of numbers. "I need you to reschedule any meetings on the book and hold my calls until I tell you different...okay...thanks!"

"I see I'm not the only one who holds calls to handle important business," I joked.

He laughed and gave me a curt nod. "Follow me into the coders' office, and let's look at this program."

The software was thoroughly explained to Mr. Bromage and his staff three hours later. Accompanying directions were discussed with Mr. Bromage and his management team. His team navigated through the different systems within the first thirty minutes without much assistance. The design was vibrant and seamless, and everyone was pleased. My team, along with the help of Lissa's company, had created a masterpiece.

I patted myself on the back as I walked out of Mr. Bromage's office with a six-figure check and the promise to use our licensed software for more new and established offices.

I dialed Lissa's number to tell her the good news. She answered on the second ring. "How did it go?" she asked, her excitement barely contained.

"Knocked it out of the park. He's bought licenses for their network and will use the software for all new offices to come," I said, with a smile that could stretch from Georgia to Alabama.

"This is celebration-worthy," she said before I had the chance to ask her to dinner.

"That's why I called to ask you out to dinner," I said.

"Give me about an hour and I'll meet you somewhere. Where do you want to go?" she asked.

"Meet me at Debonair's on Parkway Drive."

"I'll see you there in thirty," she hung up.

I called Shalonda and asked her to set everything up for our late lunch date. I also invited her to join us since she helped to make this success possible. Shalonda had a doctor's appointment that she couldn't miss, so she declined my offer. Lissa and I would be dining alone. That was a prospect I wasn't disappointed about at all.

I drove to the bank to deposit Bromage's check and to have one drawn up for Lissa.

When I walked into Debonair's thirty-five minutes later, Lissa looked stunning at our reserved table. I stood by the bar and stared at her. She wore another of her signature navy blue dresses with an oversized red belt that fit snuggly around her small waist. She sat poised, tapping her red heels against the tile floor and sipping on a mimosa. Her lips wrapped around her straw, leaving traces of her golden gloss. What I wouldn't give to be the soda flowing through her straw, being sucked up inside of her, and becoming one with her.

I shook that notion and used mind over matter to will the erection burgeoning in my slacks back under control. Finally, I moved in her direction. "Do you mind if I join you?" I asked with the sneer of a winner.

"Don't mind if you do," she stood and extended her arm for a quick hug.

I placed a drink order and told her about Bromage's reaction to the software. "He was impressed by the colorful design that you came up with. That was the most creative design I have ever seen, so I know it will be a popular draw."

"Well, I'm glad he liked it," she said humbly.

111

"Are you ready to take over the game?" I asked and raised my glass to hers.

She lifted her glass and clanked it to mine. "I just want to do what I love. It feels good to be paid for my talents."

"In doing what you love, you have no option but to be at the top because no one else can do you better than you, Lissa," I told her.

"You're right. I'm trying," she said, offering me a modest smile.

"I get you're humble, but don't you do it to be the best?"

"We all have different reasons, I assume." Her gaze left mine for far too long. I couldn't tell what was on her pretty little mind. I sat my glass down on the table and peered at her. The brilliant beauty sitting across from me intrigued me. How could she make it so far and not know that she's the best of the best?

"What's your reason?" I asked.

She placed her glass down and looked into my eyes. "To prove that I don't need to depend on a man," she said bluntly. "And plus, I've always been creative. When people saw things in black and white, I could envision the colors blended in. I knew the patterns that would make it pop and could imagine a blank canvas a thousand ways."

"Yeah, I can see that about you. Your eyes lit up when I gave you the general idea for the holistic software and what you came up with was amazing."

She took a sip of her wine. "It just comes to me all at once, and I can see it as clear as day. I only have to snap that picture in my mind and get it coded into actual software."

"The technical part is probably where it's less fun, right?"

"Yep," she laughed. "I figured by this point in my life, I would have moved to China with the man of my dreams to start a tech empire and raise a family, but this stuff apparently takes time," she said sarcastically.

"Oh, yeah? Why not start your empire in America? Why move to China?" I asked.

"Come on, it's a techie's dream, the technology superpower of the world. I think I would be in heaven there with all the next-generation thinkers."

"Well, you will definitely need a man if you want to move there with the man of your dreams," I countered, bringing up her statement about not needing a man earlier.

"When I started to focus the most on my business, I had gone through something that left me needing to prove to myself that I didn't need a man. Now, I'm ready for whoever God sends to me. I'm ready for the next step now," she shared.

"I can see that happening for you." I smiled. "I can see you accomplishing both of those goals...or any goal you set out to achieve."

There was a long pause, and we both took sips from our drinks.

"What about you? What's your reason for opening your business and going out and landing juggernaut deals like you do? You have established a well-known and respected business with high integrity, which says a lot about you." She gave me her full attention as she awaited my answer.

"My family." I pushed my drink to the side and fiddled with my silverware. "You want to move to China and start a family. I decided to start a business for my wife and two children. With my degree, I could have easily gotten a cushy, high-paying job, and we would have lived well, but I started True Colors Technology because I wanted to leave a legacy for my children. I wanted to build something that would feed my offspring for years. I envisioned doing what I did today hundreds of times over and growing a big company. I grinded day and night. I stayed up on the industry, networked and worked my ass off, and, yeah, it took time."

"From the looks of things, you have accomplished your goals. You should be proud," she said.

"I'm proud of the business," I stated truthfully.

I just didn't have much to be proud of outside of the confines of True Colors Tech. The very people I worked for fled the state to lead the life I imagined for them without me in the picture. The wealth I worked so hard to achieve was handed to Jacob when he was born, and what was his reward? My family. I worked hard and ended up without anyone to share it with. What a shitty deal!

Concern etched into the soft features of her face. "Well, why does it seem you're unsatisfied with what you've accomplished? Like there's so much competing for space in your mind?"

Was it that obvious? "I'm contemplating my next move. I always stay a step ahead of new blood, looking to come along, review our software, and one-up me using my own creation as

114

a template," I shifted the subject to something more comfortable, and I was thankful she went along with me.

"Been there before, but you know what they say? The only reward for hard work...."

"Is more hard work," I cut in, finishing her sentence.

She took another sip of her drink and agreed. "Don't I know it?"

"Are you ready to order?" I asked.

She nodded. "Yes! I thought you'd never ask. I'll be drunk before the food gets to the table at the rate I'm going."

"Well, let's get this party started." I waved our waitress over to place our order.

Lissa
Close Call

"I had a lot of fun with you today. So much fun that I don't want it to end." I stopped just before adding that I didn't want to be alone. I didn't do desperate. It had to be the mimosas talking since I had no problem admitting to Montie that I wanted to spend more time with him. We had already spent the evening together, sitting at the restaurant laughing and talking for hours.

"I had fun with you, too. When you warm up, you really have a good sense of humor, Lissa." A grin crept upon his cheeks, causing an adorable crease. "Like when you told the waiter that knock-knock joke, I thought I was going to die of laughter because of how silly you were," Montie cracked up, reminding me of how carefree I allowed myself to be with him.

"I'm sure I made a fool of myself," I giggled.

"No, it was cute, actually. I like that about you. You don't mind exposing your fun side."

"So, do you mind if we go for a walk? I'll tell you more jokes," I probed.

He stared into my eyes. I was sure he was considering if he wanted to spend more personal time with his colleague with whom he'd just signed a lucrative contract. I weighed the same thought, and my desire to be in his presence longer won.

"I mean, if you don't want to, that's fine. I have a good book to read at home," I pushed back my invite to avoid his rejection. "I just thought it would be better to talk to an actual human for a while longer," I admitted while running my hand slowly up and down my bare arms.

Montie took off his jacket and wrapped it around my shoulders to ward away the April night's air. Again, a slight dimple creased his right cheek as he smiled. I should've run in the opposite direction the first time my panties started melting over the sight of that dent. Instead, I moved even closer to where he stood and waited for his answer to my offer.

"I didn't have anything but cleaning my patio planned for this evening. I'd much rather spend my time in the presence of a pretty woman who's smart and hilariously funny."

I patted him on the shoulder as the effects of the mimosas kicked in a little more. "Don't you flirt with me."

"Okay," he shrugged his shoulders. "If you say so."

"Aw, you give up so quickly," I laughed.

"You're too much, Lissa."

We began walking toward my car.

"I just like to have fun when I'm not working. Apparently, that hasn't been often." Enjoying the moment like this was well overdue.

Montie scanned the area, looking at the random people walking around. "How about we walk in my neighborhood? It's pretty safe there," he offered.

"That's fine by me," I accepted.

"Follow me. I don't live far from here."

Anywhere, I thought as "sure" slipped easily from my mouth.

*****

"I can do the whop and the cabbage patch better than you," I said and doubled over with cackles when Montie started rolling his shoulders to do the cabbage patch.

We had walked for an hour around his quiet neighborhood, and I house- and people-watched while we got to know more about each other. We discussed what we wanted out of the future to avoid getting deep into our pasts.

I found that Montie wanted nothing more than to be an outstanding father to his children, and watching his passion as he talked about them, let me know that he already was. I didn't have any children, so I couldn't opine on the feeling of being a parent unless you count the unspeakable joy I had for my godchildren.

When it came time for me to talk about myself, I told him of one of my well-kept secret joys, my love of dancing. That's

118

how our dance-off began. Standing there watching Montie's cabbage patch was funnier than my knock-knock jokes.

"I thought you said you could dance," Montie challenged. He started kicking toward me, engaging me in a Kid and Play footwork battle. I joined him, and we kicked. Our feet interlocked, and we spun around.

"What just happened?" I asked when he ended up with his arm around my waist, pulling me to stand straight up. "Did your house just shift, or is the earth moving?" Either one meant I needed to lay my drunk tail down.

"You almost fell when we spun around."

"Good catch," I said and touched the side of my head, still spinning in circles.

"Come on, let's sit down a minute. You had quite a few mimosas at the restaurant, and now you're drinking more wine." He picked up the almost empty bottle of red wine on his table to show me how much I'd drank alone.

"Remind me not to drink like a sailor at a restaurant and then follow a man home and start drinking at his home." I sounded a little slower than usual.

"Let me get you a glass of water," he offered.

"I appreciate it, but no thanks. I think I need to go on to the house...my house, that is."

"Let me drive you. It's not a good idea that you drive tonight."

"I'll be fine."

"Yes, you will because I'll drive you."

"No, Montie." I steadied myself to prove I could make it home without an escort. "I don't want to have to go through the trouble of having to come back to get my car. I'm fine, for real."

"Well, I'm going to follow you to make sure you make it safely then." He trailed behind me to the counter, where I picked up my purse. "Let me do that, so I don't feel like a puss."

"I'm telling you, none of that is necessary. I'll be fine." I reached into my purse and took out my car keys. "I can handle driving. Everything will be just dandy," I said, recognizing my slur for the first time that night.

From the look on his face, he recognized it too.

Dang, he's going to take my keys.

"Are you sure you're fine, Lissa?" Montie asked with a sly grin.

I raised my hand over my heart as I walked to the door. "Girl Scout's honor."

"If you're fine, why are you trying to stick your key into my front doorknob?"

I looked down at my right hand hovering over his doorknob with my key. "Oh, damn. Yeah... I might need you to drive me," I regretfully admitted.

"Yeah, so like I said, I'll take you home." Montie grabbed his key from the hook, and we both laughed. Elation of that type was new to me, foreign even. It felt good to be in the presence of someone that didn't take themselves too seriously like Seth and Jameson. I appreciated a man even more who enjoyed my sense of humor without trying to take advantage of me by getting me into his bed at the end of the night.

The ride home seemed to happen in slow motion. I thought about how nice of a time I had working with Montie and getting to know the man behind the success story. He was fun and lively. He had hopes and dreams that had been deferred, just like I had. And, yes, he was all man.

I stole glimpses of his hard chest and imagined it pressed into my back when he guided me out of the restaurant. I thought of how his strong hand grabbed mine when he wanted to take a detour from the normal walking path—definitely, all man.

He pulled into my usual parking space in front of my townhouse; I reached for my purse and realized I had forgotten to zip it back up when I got my keys out earlier. Great, now everything had spilled out onto the floor.

"Aw, man," I pouted and spent a few seconds fiddling around, trying to put all my contents back inside.

"Did you get everything?" He reached across my lap to look for himself. His hand rode up my thigh as he felt around for loose objects.

I giggled at the feel of his close contact. "I'm really not that drunk, you know? I just dropped some things, but I picked them up already," I acknowledged his intrusion into my space. I looked at him as he stared at me, our lips only inches apart. If he wanted to kiss me, pretending to look for my lost items was the hard way around.

Montie slowly raised his hands up in the air and moved back into his seat. That wasn't what I wanted him to do. What I wanted him to do was to press his lips into mine, push my head against the headrest of his car, and drive me fucking insane. Obviously, he had the good sense not to ruin our working relationship in that way.

I reluctantly followed his lead with the plan to get into my house, take a cool shower, and forget I ever wanted to be Montie's thot for a night. I reached for the door handle.

"I'll get that," he jumped out and came around to open my door.

When I stepped out of the car, I looked into his dark gaze, glazed over with the moon's reflection. "Um, thank you for giving me a ride home," I muttered, the sweet smell of wine emanating from my breath and permeating the air amid us.

"I wouldn't have had it any other way. Now, let me walk you to the door."

I unenthusiastically put one foot in front of the other and sauntered to my porch. Montie shadowed close on my heels. I put my key in the door and spun around to say, "Good night."

His wet and succulent lips inched close to mine. I couldn't tell if gravity was shifting on me or if he was about to kiss me. Entrapped in the sensation of gratified anticipation, I stood frozen under Montie's intense stare. So much for my year of Yes to No. If he were to kiss me, there would be no backing away. There would be no saying No.

Were the liquor effects driving me insane, or was overdue loving that would—without a doubt—end up in heartbreak in my cards?

I pushed the ramifications of both out of my mind. My head tilted, and my mouth opened to accept the passionate intimacy I imagined awaited me on Montie's lips.

Once Montie was close enough to breathe for me, he stopped. "Thanks again for everything, Lissa," bellowed out of him with a sudden flash of innocence in his eyes.

He didn't know he'd just taken my soul out of my body and held it in his eyes. He was breathing for me just moments ago like he didn't know.

Unable to say anything, I stared at him as he continued, "I really hate that our time together has ended. I will call you soon. I'll need to use your firm again. Oh, and I'll have your car to you first thing in the morning."

I closed my mouth, righted my head, and shook off the rejection in my gut. I had been foolish to think we were more than two colleagues getting to know one another. Montie was about his business. I needed to climb out of my feelings and do the same.

"I look forward to working with you again," I managed to say, then fumbled with my key and unlocked my door. "I had fun tonight," I babbled on.

"Good night," we said together.

I stepped over my threshold and slammed the door in his handsome face, leaving him standing there looking at my door.

After I got my composure, I peeked through the blinds and watched him stand at the edge of the porch, staring at my door like he wanted to knock it down and claim me. He stood there in contemplation for at least one full minute before he turned and jogged down the steps.

Lissa
The Past Is Just That

I'd never been so happy to see my friend's face light up on my cell. "Shayla! Honey, I'm so stoked that you called. I've been needing to talk to you."

"Oh...kay...," she drawled out. "What did I miss?"

"A lot since you've been antisocial the past week," I reminded her.

"I'm sorry. I'm not trying to ignore my best friend. I've just been pregnant with my second child in a constant baby-induced sleeping coma," Shayla huffed and complained.

I giggled at how beautiful baby girl Glory would be once she arrived. "In that case, I forgive you. God-baby number two is going to be trouble. She's letting you have it right now."

"Yes, she is going to be a little booger. I have literally slept the past four months straight. And Tyler can't wait until she's here. He's always questioning me about my belly growing and her arrival. Between Tyler's questioning and Antonio's overprotectiveness, I'm over it. I can't wait to get on the delivery table. Anyway, why are you so *stoked* that I called? What's going on with you?"

"I went on a date with one of my colleagues. It started as a dinner to celebrate a successful project, and then...." I paused.

Shayla chimed in. "You screwed him."

I gasped. "Is that the best you can think of me?" I asked in a faux incredulous tone before an onslaught of giggles erupted from my throat. "No, I didn't wrestle him down and take his eggplant from him, if that's what you're thinking. That's not to say the man didn't have my panties on fire."

"Fast tail."

"At least I'm trying to behave because let me tell you...." Images of Montie standing in front of me looking like honey poured into a Brooks Brother suit flashed in my head. "It's hard not to just reach out and touch him."

"Is this the same guy you told me about last week?"

"Yes, Lord. Honey, do you remember how crazy I was about Seth when he took to the podium?"

"How can I forget?"

"Then Jameson had me on fire shortly after him. Both men almost ruined me when they left me alone. I'm trying not to get too caught up with Montie because he's ten times sexier than both, and he's open and honest about his relationship status. How much chill can a sista have in this situation?"

"Just remember Seth had a wife, and Jameson ran off with another woman Rhonda, of all people," Shayla recapped. "That's enough chill to last for a few more years, at least."

Anger rose in me at just the thought of Rhonda. "Don't even mention that wicked witch of the south's name."

"I'm just saying that she could be re-clothed in the next woman, waiting to devastate your world with secrets," Shayla exhaled. "You know I don't want it to be true for you, but that's how relationships can go."

"You've been extra blunt during this pregnancy," I pointed out.

"After everything I went through with Rhonda, I cannot help but be cynical. She ran off with my first husband and tried to trap my second with a baby. I loved her and Titus once, and they double-crossed me. Then, she used my insecurities from that marriage and tried to plant them in my second one. I think that's enough to make anyone blunt."

"It's funny how both of our men, Titus and Jameson, had a thing for her crazy tail. I would have thought more of Jameson, though. He really surprised me. As a grown-ass man, he should have gotten over his crush long ago, especially after discovering what kind of woman she was. The man is a paid courtroom bulldog, a preacher's kid, and still a sap in a puppy love that never let him go after all these years."

"He was one of the good ones corrupted by that crazy love." Shayla kissed her teeth. "Mark my words. Rhonda will show him better than anyone that it was his loss leaving you," she pointed out. The sound of a spoon scraping an empty bowl joined her voice on the line.

"I guess you have a point there. What are you eating?"

"It's gone now, but I was eating walnut ice cream. And before you get started, the walnuts are good for me."

I thought about the new set of chubby cheeks I'd be squeezing in a few more months. "I'm sure it's all good for the baby. She needs dessert too," I agreed.

"Yes, my baby is going to love sweets. But as for Rhonda, I just can't believe how she got off so easy in court," Shayla said. "She's over there in the psych hospital fooling all the nurses. Everyone who knows her knows that she's as deceitful as they come," she ruminated over her friend turned arch enemy.

"Yeah, she'll be out soon on good behavior," I agreed. "And when she is, we'll be pistol ready."

She let out a helpless sigh. "Lord, I pray for the world once she is released."

"How is Antonio doing?"

"He's been overcompensating for all the trouble Rhonda caused. I keep telling him he hasn't done anything wrong and doesn't owe me any special attention, but I love it. I don't have to lift a finger around here."

"Pregnant women always get the good treatment. I wish I had a man in my life who wanted to give me a baby. My clock is ticking, and I'm ready to have some babies."

"What about the man you just went on a date with?"

"Oh him? Lord, we would have the most gorgeous babies."
I imagined cute little brown children, a girl and twin boys,
running around a playground with Montie and me in their trails.

Laying Montie down for a night of breeding that neither of
us would soon forget was the next thing that flashed through
my mind.

"I would let him put all his babies in me," I admitted.

"Dang, he's that good, huh?"

"What I know of him is amazing. I would like to find out
more, though."

"What are you waiting on? You normally would have at
least tested the waters by now. I don't know whether to be
stunned by your cautiousness or proud."

"If I'm real about how I feel about him physically, I want
nothing more than to hop in bed with him. It gets harder and
harder to fight my attraction as each day passes. I'm not ready
to cross that line, though. We work together, and I depend on
our partnership for my firm to make money."

"Yeah, and we both know sex clouds judgments. I'd hate to
see you let it get in the way of meeting your goals."

It pained me to do it, but I reflected on Seth again. "Right,
look at what happened with Seth. I went to his conference to
learn the steps to take my company to multi-millionaire status
and ended up learning a new sexual position in his bed instead.
Sleeping with him was the biggest setback of my adult life. The
sex wasn't worth as much as I thought it was at the time."

Shayla agreed, "There definitely are more important
things."

"Yeah, you would say that with your belly full of your husband's lovechild," I teased. "When are you not having sex?"

"Hey, I can't help it that I'm always pregnant."

"Antonio won't give that booty a break."

"And I don't want one either!" Shayla cracked me up as she snapped her fingers and laughed with me.

"And yet you call me fast tail. I think we need to reevaluate our labels."

"Whatever, I have to get out of this house. When are we going to hang out again?" she whined.

"If you're awake during lunchtime tomorrow, let's do lunch."

"Sounds good to me. I'll call around eleven."

"Okay, honey. See you then."

"Bye, sweets."

Montie
Hungry for More

"Thanks for another great workout, Mario. Now, I gotta go find some grub because a brother is starving," I said as I tossed my backpack over my shoulder.

"Yo man, I hear they have good food at that new joint, The Tavern. Want to go check it out?" Mario asked.

"Only if you can leave now. My breakfast was too light to wait on your slow footing around. Let's do this if you can roll in the next two minutes. If not, I'll have to leave you behind."

"Aight, man. Calm down. I know you get cranky when you're hungry. I'm coming right out now. Just let me grab my wallet." Mario reached under the counter to unlock a door to retrieve his wallet. "You driving?" he asked.

"Nah, you might as well grab your keys, bro. You're driving today," I said.

"That's cool. I didn't want to be cramped up in your little car anyway," he said of my BMW i8. He walked toward his truck parked in his parking space by the entrance and said, "We're riding in a man's vehicle."

I hopped into his Ford F-150 that glided through Atlanta traffic like it owned the roadways. Within minutes, we pulled up to The Tavern—a nice, swanky restaurant that I noted was jam-packed once we entered. "Man, I don't feel like waiting hours to be seated and get my food. If they say it's going to take too long, I'm just going to a burger joint."

"I know you're not up in here talking about burgers to your physical trainer," Mario said.

"I sure as hell am," I said as a hostess approached us. "I can have a burger. My abs are tighter than yours. You're the one that needs to watch what you eat."

"How many?" the waitress asked, interrupting before Mario could reply with a quip.

"First, how long is your wait?" I asked in a grouchy tone.

The hostess went into saleswoman mode. "Oh, it's only about fifteen minutes on food today. We're busy, but the kitchen is moving fast."

"Cool. It's just the two of us then," I said and blew out a sigh of relief. My stomach took that time to release a roaring grumble.

"Greedy ass," Mario jested under his breath as we followed behind the hostess. Suddenly, he stopped walking and stood looking toward the back of the restaurant. "This must be my lucky day," he said as he raised his hand to his mouth and blew into it. He took a whiff and smiled in satisfaction with his findings.

132

"What is it? Did you find a buffet?" Looking for delicious, prepared food, I trained my eyes on the edge of the room that he was staring in.

"Look to the right, second table. I'm about to go holler at the one in the blue dress and see what's up," Mario said and motioned his head toward a table in the center of the restaurant where, no doubt, a magnificent woman sat with a very pregnant woman.

"Aye," I tried to catch Mario. He rubbed his hands together and dapped off like a reincarnated Superfly from the 70s. Mario was already at the table talking to Lissa when I caught up with what was happening.

It was a month after our business dinner/date. I thought about her continuously when we weren't working on a tech design project. I recounted the jokes she told on our first date and laughed at them repeatedly, reflecting on my time with her.

Now, my homeboy was trying to push up on her. I must admit, it was a pleasure to see her smile nervously as she talked to Mario. I'd only known her for a few weeks, but we had gotten comfortable with each other in that short period of time.

I hung back just to see how she responded to Mario. She was cordial. However, she didn't look interested in taking him up on anything he offered. That was evident when she shook her head with her eyes squinted like she was trying to figure him out. He placed his fingers on his chin and rubbed at the stubble growing there as he tried to get her to lighten up. She didn't. He looked like he was sweating in the hot seat, and I relished every minute of his torture.

I walked over to help Mario escape the awkward situation he'd gotten himself into. "I couldn't help but notice you two beautiful ladies sitting here peacefully until my friend decided to badger you. I came over to save you from him. He's really just a nice guy who knows two beautiful ladies when he sees them," I said.

Mario smirked. "Yeah, I do know beautiful women when I see them."

"Hi there," Lissa squeaked out, then stood to hug me. "So good to see you again," she added before she returned to her seat. "Would you like to join us like your friend, Mario, already has?"

"Nah, you two ladies enjoy yourself. Mario and I would hate to interrupt your lunch date," I said, knowing Mario had already intruded.

"No, you're perfectly fine," the pregnant woman said as she sent questioning gazes from me to Lissa. "If you're a friend of Lissa's, you're a friend of mine."

"Montie, this is Shayla—Shayla, Montie." Lissa introduced us. "And she's right; we don't mind you joining us."

I shook Shayla's hand and introduced Mario. "This is my friend Mario."

"Oh, we've met Mario," Lissa giggled. A wild, heated glance passed between Lissa and me when our eyes locked.

"Hi Mario," Shayla spoke, checking us both out. She studied Lissa, who was having as much trouble as I was hiding her attraction to me.

"Hey," Mario answered. His enthusiasm when he strutted over to their table in full confidence that he would be picking Lissa up had fizzled away. It was obvious by the bun in Shayla's oven that she was taken. That left Mario without anyone to score.

"How are you doing this afternoon?" I addressed the question to both ladies, but my eyes were glued to Lissa's. Her smooth mocha brown skin coated with a hint of shimmer shined bright under the restaurant's lighting. I didn't think she could be any prettier. She somehow managed to highlight every aspect of her natural beauty, down to the glistening pink gloss of her lips.

"I'm fine. How are you, Montie?" she asked with a blush rising upon her cheek as I took the seat next to her. I thought it had been the liquor after our date that made that smile appear, but that wasn't it. I was intrigued.

"I'm having a great day now," I replied. "Have you guys ordered yet?"

"Yeah, because my man here is starving," Mario interjected. "I'm sure he'll be ready to go if the food is not out in ten minutes, right, Montie?"

"No, I can wait," I shot Mario a glare that let him know to chill out.

"That's good to hear," he said with a slight chuckle. "Cause you said you wouldn't wait longer than fifteen minutes when we came in here."

"That was then. Now, I'll wait on the food, however long it takes," I said, narrowing my eyes at him. He threw his hands up in neutrality, looked at Lissa, and then back at me. Now, both Mario and Shayla were scrutinizing us with their questioning gazes.

"So, how do you two know each other?" Shayla broke the loud silence.

"Montie is the owner of True Color Technology, the company I closed the deal I was telling you about last week."

Shayla's right brow rose. "Oh, so this is Mr. Brown?"

"Yes," Lissa answered.

Shayla returned to sipping on the glass of water in front of her. "Nice to meet you," she said when she placed it back on the table.

"Montie, we've already ordered. When the waitress returns, you can place your order," Lissa said as I scanned the menu.

When the waitress returned, Mario and I placed our orders. I decided on a burger and fries.

"I'll have the chicken salad," Mario told the waitress. "I'm his physical trainer who is totally appalled by the hamburger and fry thing he's doing to his body," Mario added, which caused Shayla to laugh.

"You're funny," she said.

"Yes, he is a jokester," I admitted.

136

We kept the conversation light over the next few minutes. The waitress returned to the table with a salad for Lissa, a humongous plate of fries covered with chili and cheese for Shayla, Mario's salad, and my hearty burger.

One hour later, my ravenous appetite was quenched, and I had my fill of hanging with the two beautiful, smart, and witty ladies—oh and Mario too.

"I hate to see our time together end, but I have a 3 p.m. doctor's appointment," Shayla announced as she gathered her purse.

"I guess I should go too. I have work that's not going to get done by magic," Lissa said to her friend. "I enjoyed having lunch with you, Montie."

"And what about me?" Mario pouted.

"I enjoyed your company too, Mario," Lissa said.

"You both were entertaining," Shayla threw in.

"Thanks, it was nice meeting both of you, ladies. We have to do this again sometime," Mario said.

Lissa looked in my direction. "Yes, we should meet up here again soon."

"Most definitely," I drank her in with my eyes. She wasn't getting rid of me any time soon, so we would definitely meet up here again.

She let out a slight moan that sent a surge of energy through me. Then, her brown eyes scanned the room. "Where is the waitress with our ticket?"

I pointed to the kiosk in the center of the table. "I already settled the tab, so we're good."

"Montie, you didn't have to pay for our food. We could have gotten it," Lissa said.

Mario helped Shayla wobble from her chair to a rocky stand.

"Yeah, we could have paid, but thanks," Shayla agreed.

"It's really not a problem at all. What kind of a man do you think I am? Of course, I bought you two beautiful ladies' lunches. This was the highlight of my day." Helping Lissa from her seat, I added, "And, we must get together soon to spend more time together when we're not working on projects."

"Oh, so your workout wasn't the highlight of the day? I'm crushed," Mario pouted again.

I shot him a glare telling him to knock it off. "Really, Mario?"

Lissa giggled and started walking to the exit. Salivating over her every stride, I shadowed her out to the curbside. She hugged Shayla, and Shayla shook mine and Mario's hands.

"Again, nice meeting you," Shayla said before walking to her car.

"The pleasure is all mine," I said as I stared into Lissa's light brown eyes.

"Wow, Atlanta is always growing. They're just building up all around here," Mario admired a funkily painted building to the right of The Tavern. "Is that a new pool hall?" he asked.

"I never noticed it there before, but yeah, that's a pool hall," Lissa said, surveying the building.

"If you had time, I'd take you in there and whoop you in a few games," I challenged her.

She glared at me. "Is that a challenge, Montie Brown?"

"It was more of a promise. But you said you had a lot of work to do. I'd hate you to get behind on your work and whipped all in one day, so we can do it some other time."

"Well, in the case of all of your trash-talking, my schedule just cleared up so I can teach you a hard lesson about threatening to beat this girl in pool," she accepted my challenge with a competitive arch of her brow.

"Are y'all about to go in there for real?" Mario asked.

"Yeah, come on with us. You can be the witness to her tragic loss," I said.

"I can't stay. I have a training session at 2 p.m.," he said.

"Dang, that's right. I left my car at the gym and rode with Mario. Looks like I'm going to need to take a raincheck, Lissa."

"I could give you a ride to get your car. That's if you don't mind riding back with the girl that's kicked your tush in pool," Lissa bragged.

"I can't wait to put you in your place," I said, taking her by the hand. "I'll catch up with you later, Mario," I tossed over my shoulder at my friend, who was already heading to his car.

"And where exactly is my rightful place?" Lissa asked once we reached the door of the pool hall.

"Once I win, I get to pick where we go on our next date. Then, I'll show you your place better than I can explain it to you," I said.

"Oh, wow, so we're dating?"

"Well, we've been hanging out for sure. Maybe it would be better if we called it a business date," I suggested.

"Do I get the same thing? If I win, do I get to choose our next business date?" she asked.

"That's the wager. Whoever wins gets to choose our next hang-out spot," I confirmed.

"That way, no matter who wins, we get the same thing. How is that a fair wager?" she asked.

"That's fair, but when I win, you have no idea of the places I will take you," I uttered before I could catch myself. Being around Lissa made me comfortable. She felt familiar, like someone I'd known for years.

She gasped, and her hand flew to her mouth. I knew then that I'd gotten just a little too comfortable too fast. "Is that another threat, Montie?" she asked with a raised brow.

Whether we would end up just working together, friends or lovers, I decided then and there to just be honest. "I told you where I stand on threats. I don't make them. I make promises."

We walked in and chose a table. Lissa leaned against the table and bit down on her lip. "Well, what if I win?" she asked in a raspy tone that nearly made me unglued.

I placed the balls in the middle of the table and thought about the ravenous little fireball curved to perfection. "*If* you win, and that's a strong if, then I will take you anywhere you want to go in the world," I said as a guarantee.

Lissa arched her back so that her torso dipped close to the table, leaving nothing to imagine about how her rounded, plump ass would spread out in my bed. "Put your money where your mouth is, Montie."

Glory. She was a beautiful sight. She revved her pool stick backwards and hit the first strike sending the balls flying in different directions on the table and shoving my salacious thoughts to the back of my mind.

Three in the pockets. *Impressive.*

"Good start," I congratulated her, "but don't get used to it. That's all the points you'll get this game."

We ended up playing two rounds, with Lissa stomping me each time. She really was a good pool player. Thankfully, I had set the rules so that I won, no matter how the game turned out. We were going on another date.

"If we are going to be seeing more of each other, you must get used to me winning," Lissa bragged as she drove toward Mario's gym, so I could pick up my car.

"If I can set the rules so that we both win, I don't care if you win," I admitted.

"So, you think you'll like our next date, huh? How do you know I will not take you somewhere and work you like a slave?" she forewarned.

"As long as I'm with you, I'm down for whatever."

That caused her plump lips to stretch into a delicious spread across her face. "Good, I'll text you the address to the place tonight. I want you to meet me there at 6 p.m. sharp tomorrow evening."

Montie
The Next Day

I turned onto Washington Street and assessed the empty buildings on both sides of the road. Lissa must have given me the wrong address. There was no restaurant in sight and no place that looked even remotely decent enough to have a date. I pulled over and parked in front of a meter alongside the road in front of an old, dilapidated church and dialed her number.

"Hello," her melodic voice chimed through the phone, brightening my mood instantly. Even if she had given me the wrong address, I could never be upset with her.

"Hey, Lissa."

"Hey, where are you?"

"I'm out here on Washington. I don't see a restaurant anywhere near the address you gave me. My GPS brought me to what looks like a rundown church." I looked at the building again and down the street in front of me. A few cars were parked outside, but I couldn't figure out which of the buildings those people might've been congregated in.

"No worries, Montie. You're in the right place. I'm coming out to get you now," she beamed out with excitement.

"So, this is it? I'm in the right place?" I asked, confused as I continued to look down the street in front of me. I thought surely she would come out of a quaint building that I missed in my surveillance of the area. There had to be an unknown Atlanta hot spot hiding in this worn area.

"Yes. This is it, Montie," she said sweetly as the door of the church opened. She stepped out wearing a warm smile.

"Oh, I see you at the top of the steps," I acknowledged as the paltry surroundings faded and her beauty became all I could see. I paused to watch her delicate features as she smiled back at me. Lissa was one show-stopping woman.

She waved me over. "Come on in. This is where we'll be hanging out tonight."

I joined her on the steps just outside the church door. "This is what you have planned for our date?" I asked with the faintest hint of disappointment in my tone. If her idea of a date was having a pastor standing over us preaching on a Tuesday night, the hours ahead would be a serious test.

I popped a piece of chewing gum in my mouth and stared at her soft brown eyes. They held the power to send calming vibes all over me. I did prefer to be wherever she was going to be, doing whatever she was doing over sitting at home sulking over my past. *But this place?*

143

She stood on her tiptoes and graced my lips with a quick peck. "Just come in with me, Montie."

I licked my lips to savor the flavor of her sweet gloss.

"We'll be helping others for the rest of the night, so consider that kiss your service prepayment." She chortled.

I smiled at her. "Okay. That was a nice-sized payment."

"This'll be the best date anyone has ever taken you on. I promise you that," she assured me as she pulled me toward the door.

A fair warning was warranted, so I told her, "Lissa, I like you a lot, but I don't want you to be upset with me if I go in here and decide this church isn't for me. I don't comingle with judgmental or over preachy people."

"Montie, I wouldn't bring you to a place like that," she said. "Granted, you don't know me that well, but I thought you, at least, knew me better than that."

"Let's see...what do I know? You're funny, smart, highly successful, and so damn beautiful with the biggest set of kissable lips that I have ever tasted and that's not to mention your ass...."

An elderly couple made it to the top of the steps.

Lissa coughed to stop me from speaking.

"Let me get that for you." I held the door open so they could walk in ahead of us.

"Thanks, Son," the man said as he entered the door.

"No problem." I smiled at the lady who reminded me of my grandmother. Once the couple was inside, I finished my statement. "Like I was saying, not to mention your assets."

Lisa laughed. "If I didn't know any better, I would say that you were getting frisky with me."

I smiled mischievously. "We're at a church, Lissa. I wouldn't dare."

"I think what we're doing tonight will help us get to know each other better. I want you to know this side of me. Give me a chance to show you without judgment, and if you don't like what you see, you can walk away, no strings attached."

Without knowing what waited inside, I didn't realize the implications of what she was saying to me. However, I had no intention of walking away from her. If nothing else, we had a long business relationship ahead of us.

I opened the door to the church and allowed her to walk in front of me. As soon as we reached the sanctuary, I noticed a line of people wrapped around the room, leading to a backroom. "What's going on here?" I asked.

"Tonight, we serve the people." She took my hand and walked me down the church aisle to the back, where she handed me an apron and a pair of gloves. "I have you working mac and cheese. We give them a small scoop each because, by the end of the night, we will have served a thousand people, give or take."

"Are you saying I'll scoop one thousand hunks of mac and cheese?" I gasped in surprise at her revelation that our date had shifted in intent much too fast for me to comprehend. People served my food to me at restaurants. I had never worked an assembly line serving food to the community.

"Well, there are two lines with the same thing on each side, so maybe five hundred," she laughed. "I'll be right beside you, giving out green beans."

I had gotten dressed in some of my best casual wear and was well shaven with new clean-smelling cologne and a fresh haircut for my time with Lissa. I anticipated a five-star meal and a walk by the riverside.

When I was sure I had seen four hundred and ninety-nine smiles on the people's faces and the humbleness with which they came to receive food from a rundown church that I didn't even know existed, I was sold. Anything I felt for Lissa got real in that instance. I was in love with her spirit by the night's end. I loved that woman for everything she stood for when I scooped my last serving of mac and cheese and looked at her work tirelessly with a smile as she raised her last scoop of green beans.

We could've been anywhere. She could have used this time to make a hundred-thousand-dollar deal with a potential client or be wined and dined at an expensive restaurant. Still, she chose to look into the eyes of those less fortunate and light them up with her smile and loving spirit, and she brought me along to experience it. I was beyond taken by her. I was always preaching about doing what mattered. She showed me that it was more fulfilling to just *do* what mattered.

"Glad you didn't run out on me," she said as she came out of the kitchen with a large utility broom in her hand and began sweeping. "It wasn't that bad, was it?"

"I'm definitely worn out, but—"

"You didn't like it." She halted, sweeping and held the broom close to her chest, her heart-melting smile fading away.

"No, this was an experience I will never forget. I loved it. Thank you for sharing this part of you with me," I said. Her lips upturned in a smile, making everything right in my world again.

"You're welcome, Montie. It brings me so much joy to give back. When I beat you at pool, I figured I had to bring you along for the weekly community dinner." Her glare dead set upon mine rendered me incapable of looking anywhere but into her pretty brown eyes. "I'm not trying to imply anything more than what we are. I understand that we're just two people doing business and getting to know one another. I just wanted to do something with you that's meaningful to me."

I cut her misunderstanding by closing the space between us and crashing my lips onto hers. I kissed her the way I wanted to since the first night we broke the first rule of engagement for business partners and went back to my place after our celebratory dinner. That night, I had been able to subdue my feelings for her because I was confused by them. But standing there in the church's kitchen, sweaty and with mac and cheese stained clothing, I was overtaken with the desire to become one with the five-foot-two beautiful soul standing in front of me.

Judging from the look in her eyes when I finally released her, our soul-burning kiss had smoothed out any rough areas her mind was taking her to. She understood completely that I was ready for whatever she wanted to share with me.

"I, uh, I think we should finish up here, so we can leave," she said and handed me the broom. "Do you mind sweeping out here?" she asked, quickly picking up a pan warmer and rushing toward the kitchen.

"Hey," I called after her.

"Yeah."

"I'm glad you won the game."

"Me too." She smiled and slipped inside the kitchen.

I stared after her knowing I had let her win the game, just like I was allowing her into my heart with each passing moment.

Lissa
Let's Fly Away

"Wow, Year of Yes was amazing from the beginning to end, Shayla. You should read it as soon as possible," I yelped with excitement over the content I spent the last month absorbing.

"Girl, you and that book. I called you so you can tell me more about Mr. Montie...not about Shonda's journey to Shondaland. Humph, I could tell from how you guys were looking at each other at the table the other day that you wanted to jump down each other's throat and extract tonsils," said Shayla.

"No, we didn't look like that."

"Are you kidding me? The fact that you want to jump each other's bones is blatantly evident to anyone standing within a half a mile radius of you two."

"What are you even talking about, Shayla?" I feigned ignorance, though the irrepressible urge to put my stamp all over Montie and brand him as mine was clear to me. I thought about our "date" at the church last night and prayed that our physical attraction wasn't obvious to the people there.

"So now you're going to sit on this phone and act like I didn't see two people salivating over one another. Okay. You tried it, Lissa."

"Well, you might have seen a lil something," I said and immediately wished I could take back the country drawl that bellowed out of me.

Shayla admonished, "The way you talk shows that he has your nose wide open. Don't start acting like a little girl in love like you did with Seth. Keep your grown woman panties on."

I sounded starstruck with my response, "I'm trying my hardest not to fall into the sunken place with Montie, but it is terribly hard. I mean, he's perfect. He loves his kids. He's kind-hearted. And the way he looks at me, honey. I melt each time his eyes feast upon me like he's starved for love. What am I going to do, Shay?"

"I know you're not asking me. The man is freaking edible. If I weren't married, humph, I might jump his bones. But let me stop while I'm ahead." Shayla chuckled.

"Yeah, you stop it. You're already pregnant, and if Antonio hears you talking about another man like that, he might give you a spanking."

"That wouldn't be such a bad thing. However, he knows I can still see how other men look. He also knows I would never touch any man but him. We're good."

150

"That's all I want in a relationship. To be good with a man who wants to keep me pregnant, like you and Antonio." I laugh. "I want a man with no excess drama, like a wife or a crazy ex. So far, Montie seems pretty stable in those categories."

"Well, every man isn't bad. I may be biased, but you're a wonderful person, Lissa. There is no way these good men will let you stay single. It would defy nature."

"Mother Nature surely isn't giving a damn about me finding a man right now."

"She sent you Montie."

"Do you think he's the one for me?"

"I think you should give him a chance. Take it slow and find out if he has any skeletons—or other women—in his closet, but definitely try him out."

"Well, this is rich. I rarely get permission from you to try a man out," I chortled as my phone vibrated against my hand. "Hey, speak of the devil, and his sexy ass will appear. Let me call you back, Shayla. This is Montie calling me now."

She squealed, "Get 'em, girl. Catch you later."

"Ha, I'll call you back later, sis." I clicked over and greeted Montie. "Hey, you. How are you doing today?"

His deep baritone flooded the line. "I'm doing good. Just working hard and thinking about you."

"Aw, that's sweet."

"What do you have planned for this evening?" he asked.

I scanned my bedroom dimmed with only a lamp. I was lying in the center of my massive king-size bed with a huge smile because I had just finished reading a good book, talked to

151

my girl, and was now flattered by Montie's deeply smooth, baritone voice. "I had nothing planned for the night but relaxation. I took the evening off to finish my book. Now that I'm done, I'll lay around and be a bum. I don't plan to even look at a computer screen for any reason," I admitted.

"You're a lucky girl. While I'm slaving over my computer, you're at home playing hooky."

"You have to give yourself time to just breathe sometimes. I skipped rest for so many years. Now that I have built my company with a dependable team, I take time off whenever I feel overstressed. Today was one of those days."

"I guess you're right. I'll pack up in a little while and get out of here, but I have something to ask you. The Tech World Order (TWO) conference is next weekend and—"

"It is?" I deflated when I thought of the date. Sure enough, the event had snuck up on me again. "Dang! I keep saying I'm going to sign up for that. Whenever it comes around, I never make plans in time. They were sold out last year when I considered it."

"What I have to ask will be pleasant news to your ears. I have two tickets and would love for you to go to Tokyo with me to the conference," he beamed.

"Wait a minute. That conference is usually sold out months in advance. How did you get two tickets on such short notice?"

"I just need to know if you want to go and if so, leave the rest to me."

"Of course, I would. It's the Mecca of software conventions."

Montie sounded pleased that I accepted his offer. "Then, say no more. I will get Shalonda to email you an itinerary for our trip, and we're out of here."

"Montie, this is too freaking much. I will owe you big time after this, for sure."

"I only have one request."

"What's that?"

"That you think of a creative way to thank me with your pretty brown lips."

I smiled so wide that my face hurt. "You have a deal."

Montie
Don't Look Back.
We're Not Going That Way

"Hey Montie, this is Destiny! I was calling because Montie Jr.'s team will be in the weekend championship game. It's All-State for the soccer tournament. He would love for you to be there, so it would be great if you could fly in. When you get a chance, give me a call back...Beep!"

My luggage was scattered about my bedroom. Lissa and I were leaving for Japan in a matter of hours. The training conference wasn't offered again until the end of the year, and the impending time alone with Lissa was the only thing that kept me going for the past week.

Destiny had gotten Montie Jr. on the team as an add on last month shortly after I left Miami. And I would have chosen the next conference date had I known my son would be playing for the All-State championship. Why in the hell was Destiny just telling me about Junior's final game?

I slammed the suitcase in my hand down onto the bed and dialed her back. Before she could answer the phone, I let her have it. "What's the deal with you just telling me about Junior's game? I have training out of the country this weekend. If you had told me sooner, I would have made other arrangements. My flight is booked for Japan in just a few hours!"

"Montie, I didn't know—"

"Nah, this long-distance shit with my children is getting played out already. When exactly did you plan to tell me about the game? That's all I want to know unless you planned to tell me when it was too late for me to come anyway."

"Montie, we didn't know they were going to make it to the championship until the game yesterday, and that's when I left you a message. That's how sports goes, you know? Besides, I told you that all the games they played until yesterday would determine whether they made All-State. You haven't come to any other games, so I figured it's not a big deal if you can't make it to this one."

"Not a big deal! Not a fucking big deal? Do you think it's not a big deal that I know my son is one game away from All-State?" I took a deep breath and sat down on the bed. I rubbed my temples and looked at the picture of my children hanging on the wall to channel whatever calm I had left. "Destiny, I call bullshit. I'm beyond pissed that I didn't know about this earlier. I know you have your nice little family thing going on, but you must remember that I am his one and only father. First and foremost, I should know about anything my kids have going on."

"Well, Montie. I'm glad you point out that you are his father because you're not acting like it. You knew he was playing to win, but when did you ever call to see how the season was going? You have gone back to your old work habits, and it's gotten to the point where you don't answer the phone for us anymore. You are too busy, just like you were when we were married. I call, but I get your voice message. I don't always leave a message, but your kids are Facetiming you and attempting to Skype you, and you're too busy to answer. So, before you hop down off your high horse and talk junk about how I'm handling our co-parenting relationship, make sure you answer your phone every time you see my number. If not, you need to be replying quickly. If you miss a Facetime, you need to return promptly. You're not the only one not getting their fair share of communication. What about you telling me you're leaving for Japan in a few hours? Don't you think I should know whether my children's father is in Atlanta or Japan?"

"Destiny, you know more than one way to get in touch with me. I'd see my kids more often if we lived in the same city. I would know what was happening with them, and you would know what's happening with me."

"We can communicate by phone, Montie."

"I just want to be at every game possible. To do that, I need you to text or email me the schedule in advance. Is that too much to ask?" She sniffled, and my tone softened. "Look, from now on, just make sure you coordinate everything through

Shalonda. She has my schedule and will ensure I don't miss a beat with my kids. If you miss me when you try to call me, get in touch with her. She will make sure that I stop what I'm doing to get back to you. It's important that this works, but we both must do our part." I must admit that some of Destiny's calls had gone to voicemail when I had been so preoccupied with spending time with Lissa or thinking about Lissa. I didn't want that to happen again.

"Fine," she sounded like the breath had been knocked out of her lungs.

We both sat on the line quiet for the next minute.

"I'm sorry. I didn't mean to come off as rude, Destiny. I'm just overwhelmed with you guys being in Miami, and yes, I have gotten back into working extra hours to fill my time. That's because I'm trying to stay sane."

Lissa's big smile crossed my mind; she had quickly become my peace in this tumultuous storm.

"Montie, I'll coordinate Junior's events through Shalonda going forward. That way, you will know when and where the games are. Some are based on how well the team does, though. I won't always have advance notice."

"That's all I want. Thank you, Destiny."

"I know you want to be here for Montie Jr. tomorrow. I will record the game and send it to you as soon as it's over," she offered.

"I would like that."

"Montie, I have something else to tell you," her voice shook as she spoke, putting me on high alert. What else was going on with her?

"Is everything okay?" I asked, concerned.

"No, it's not. Do you remember Justine?"

"Yeah." My heart rate increased, and my palms grew sweaty at the mention of Justine. I could've lived my entire life without hearing about her again, and I would be just dandy. "Jacob's ex, yeah, I remember her," I said.

"Well, she was to marry this man named Rick. On their wedding day, he left her at the altar. Justine and Jacob had been best friends since they were children, so he comforted her afterwards, and they started dating," she paused, and only heavy breathing could be heard on the line.

"What does this have to do with anything that's going on now?" I prodded.

"His...his remains were found in the woods five miles away from Justine's parents' estate."

"Whose remains, Rick's?"

"Yes. She killed him. I know she did," Destiny cried out, finally releasing the explosive tension she'd been holding since I called her. "I'm so afraid that she's going to try to do something to me or the kids. Jacob has hired extra security to be with us, but I don't know what to do to calm down."

"Has she tried to contact you?" I fished. "I mean, has she said or done anything that would make you think she's coming after you?"

"No, we haven't heard anything from her. I think that's the scariest part. It feels like the quiet before the tornado. She's a loon, and it wouldn't surprise me if she had a kill list and I was on it." I could hear the worry in her tone. Destiny was doing everything she could to hold it together.

My conscience nudged me to tell her I spent one long night screwing Justine senseless. I also needed to spill Justine's revelation about sleeping with Jacob. Honesty meant a lot to me, but Destiny had enough to worry about at the moment. Adding mine and Jacob's affairs with the deranged, lying bitch would only further devastate her.

A woman like Justine being infatuated with Destiny's life strongly indicated that she, along with Montie Jr. and Montana, was in danger. And, hell, Jacob would be the next one in the woods, lifeless if he wasn't careful.

I balled my fists into powerful knots as I growled. Justine needed to get taken down before she harmed someone I loved.

"I'm canceling my flight and coming to Miami," I barked.

"No, no. That's not necessary. We're not letting her control our lives. You have your conference to attend."

I huffed. "I won't spend the weekend worried about you guys."

"No, I won't let you cancel your plans. Go to your conference. We'll be fine. Security is on every corner of our property. Jacob is working from home and hasn't left my side since the news broke about Rick."

"Are you sure? Because if something happens to my children, it will be hell to pay, Destiny. I'm going to lose it."

"Did you forget I'm their mother? I feel the exact same way. I'm sure we'll be fine, though. I only told you about Justine because I wanted you to know what we were dealing with down here. I don't want to give her the power to stop us from living. I want you to be happy, and worrying about us will not accomplish that."

"How can I be happy while I'm worried about you and the kids? Now isn't a good time for me to leave the country. The crazy bitch will try something." The thought of disappointing Lissa weighed heavily on me, but I would do anything to protect my family.

"Montie, I can't stop living because of Justine. I just have to have faith, mace and put on a good face. And I'm ordering you to do the same thing. Go to Japan."

"Destiny," I blew out a gush of air. "I'll go if you promise to take the kids to your mother's for the time being. When I get back to the states, I'll bring them to Atlanta with me for a while."

"That's the same thing Mama said for me to do. I'm taking them over to her house after the game tomorrow. John has hired security for her too." She paused. "Thanks for caring about us, Montie," she said, and I could hear the weakness in her crumpling voice.

"You're the mother of my children. I'll always care for you and my children."

"I know."

"Call me at any time, for any reason. I'll be on the next plane smoking to Miami if you need me, okay?" I asked.

"I will. Goodbye, Montie," she said and hung up.

I sat with the phone to my ear for a long while. My heart lurched in my chest as I weighed the decision of leaving the country or flying to Miami to handle Justine myself.

My phone rang, and Lissa's face flashed on the screen.

"Hello."

"Hey Montie, I'm all packed and waiting for you to come to pick me up. I packed a few special things for you, too," she said in a bubbly tone that made me smile through the concern that had plagued me just moments before. "And don't ask me what they are because they are a surprise. I really need this time away. I'm looking forward to spending the weekend with you."

"I'll be there shortly," I answered the wavering question of whether I'd be flying to Miami or Japan. I trusted Destiny would protect our children as she had done all their lives.

"What's wrong?" Lissa asked, obviously picking up on my tone.

"Nothing, I'm just finishing up my packing, and I'll be there to get you."

"Hurry. We don't want to miss our flight. You know how crazy it can be at Hartsfield." Her voice was thick when she added, "And, I don't want to miss the opportunity to get you all alone in another country."

"Have I ever told you I appreciate how you think?" I asked.

"I think you have."

"I'm on the way."

*****

On the long flight to Japan, I confided in Lissa about my conversation with Destiny. I told her all about my marriage and our divorce. Heck, I even told her that Destiny and I had a brief rekindle before she eventually went back to Jacob. I let her know where my feelings were a few months ago and where they were now. "I thought I would never get to the point where I would be genuinely interested in another woman. However, my heart has been swept away by a spectacular thick, mocha queen who is all about her business, has a heart of gold, and put me out of my misery by agreeing to fly to Japan with me," I told her as we flew miles high in the Asian skies. "After years of living in the dark, you brought light back into my life. I don't care how long it takes. I'm going to show you that I care about you, Lissa. You just wait and see."

"Montie, I hear what you are saying. It's just that—"

"You don't want to be hurt again," I took the words out of her mouth.

She had explained to me her past two relationships with two men who didn't appreciate what they had. They gave up a breathtaking woman, and I had the honor of showing her how beautiful she was and what she deserved in a man.

"That's right, Montie. I've been through too much already with men. I just can't go down that road again."

I cast a silent prayer to God.

If this is meant to be Heavens, let me be all she needs and more.

Your boy Montie.

I brought her hand to my lips for a peck, then held it in mine. "Lissa, I just opened up and told you everything there is to know about my past. I'd never do anything to hurt you, at least not intentionally. When I'm in a relationship, I'm a one woman's man. That's where I want to be with you. You don't have to worry about having a wife like Seth; you know I'm divorced and I've told you about our situation. You damn sure don't have to worry about no childhood crushes coming back; I can't even remember anyone that could light a candle next to you."

"What about Destiny?"

"It's over for us. Anything we could have had that would have been sacred has already been tarnished by misunderstandings, third parties, and just too much pain. All this time, I thought I'd be okay if I could just get my past back. Now, I know that my true growth is in my future. I want a chance to love you the way you deserve to be loved if you will allow me to."

"All of this sounds good, but if you fucking hurt me, I'm not playing nice. I allowed the last two men to throw me away like a used rag. The next time a man treats me like that, I will be the worst bitch in heels you ever want to meet."

"Don't talk like that through your pretty lips," I said, running my finger over her luscious lips before I placed a peck on them. "There won't be a next time."

"I'm trying to be serious, Montie," she pointed out.

"Neither of us wants to be hurt again. So, let's make a pact to handle our hearts with care," I said as I inhaled the scent of

163

her puffy hair just before I converted that peck into an all-out make-out session.

*****

We made it to the hotel within an hour of the plane landing. I figured we both needed rest after the long flight. We reached Lissa's room, and she didn't stop in front of her door. She kept walking, nodding toward mine next door. The heated look in her eyes spoke to me. She longed for the very thing that kept me up at night, tossing and turning. A smile curved my lips as we passed her suite and entered my room.

The door closed behind us of its own will. I dropped the luggage I was carrying and pulled her into my arms. Her rolling bags fell to the floor as soul-grabbing kisses expressed the sweet agony of being parted from her lips for far too long. Her hands roamed the expanse of my back.

I pulled her closer to me, as close as she could get. She reached for my waist, searching for something a little more primal. She fumbled for my belt, feeling my hardness that was fully ready for her.

"Lissa, are you sure you want to do this now? We don't have to…." She tugged at my pants, which dropped to the carpet. "…rush."

"We're not rushing," she began sucking my bottom lip into her mouth. "It's almost been a month, and I've wanted to do this since the day I met you."

She stuck the pads of her fingers into my boxers and pushed them down, unleashing an erection that raged harder than ever before.

As her soft hands grasped at my thickness, I guided her to the sofa and sat down, causing her to release her firm hold of me. I gently and deliberately unbuttoned her jeans and pulled them down over her hips and all the way to her feet while she kicked off her shoes.

Her appeal was glaringly evident. She stood in front of me in a pair of fire-engine red panties, which now had a dark red wet patch starting at the tip of the triangle and continuing to the back. I smelled her fragrant arousal. Her scent was so enticing that I stopped to press my face close to her triangle as if to pull her essence inside me.

With my hands on the backs of her thighs, I pulled her panties off and yanked her down onto my lap. She clasped her ankles behind my back. I gently pulled her t-shirt off and removed her bra. She was much less gentle when she pulled off my shirt, too impatient to remove the two top buttons.

Once there was nothing between us, her hand went back to my manhood, gently stroking it all the way from my heavy scrotum that filled her hands to the base and back to its wet tip. Her soft hands felt so good on my bare skin. A sensuous groan arose from deep within my throat and I roared like a lion. My hands roamed all over her. My lips started their own exploration.

Her eyes, I looked into them deeply. Then my left hand went to the back of her neck and pulled her closer. While she closed her eyes in anticipation, I kissed each of them. I loved the shape of her nose and kissed the tip oh so gently.

My lips followed the line of her jaw to the spot under her earlobe and pressed against it for what seemed like the longest time. Her head fell back to expose her mocha neck, and I showered kisses all over it. My right hand stayed on her bottom, exploring the region from her tailbone and down.

With her on my lap, I turned and she landed underneath me. She let go of my erection and had luxurious anticipation on her gorgeous face. With my knees on the sofa, I opened her legs and bent over to reach her right breast with my mouth. My right hand stroked her left breast from the base to the juicy, erect nipple. She moaned with pleasure when I sucked her breast into my mouth, then I paid the right side the same attention.

"Baby, do you want me to make love to you?"

She nodded.

I ran two fingers across her dripping wet slit. *Glory,* her nether lips were so beautiful.

"Are you sure? I can't say I'll have any control once I start?" I asked again.

"Montie, I want you to make love to me," she murmured.

As she gyrated her heated mound against my fingers, an unbelievable amount of blood went surging to my dick. Hearing those sweet words drip from her luscious lips sent me into a heated frenzy.

My dick sat at her wet opening, and she grasped at it, hoping to pull it in and put out our raging fire once and for all.

166

In a move that stunned her, I backed away and moved further down her body, dropping kisses and nibbles in a fiery trail all the way to the core of her womanhood. She moaned and grabbed at my low-cut hair as my tongue touched her clitoris. My tongue worked its way slowly in between her lips, and her hands pushed down on my head. I flicked in a quick, steady motion across her swollen clit with no plan to stop until she was near the edge of eternity. Only then would I cram my swollen rod in her tight little hole.

"Oh, no...no...no," she begged me to stop playing in her sticky juices, much to my pleasure. "Give it to me, please, Montie," she pleaded.

Her request was music to my ears. However, nothing would stop me from slowly savoring the taste of her sweetness that I longed to taste. Her hips vainly thrust up at my face. She was about to release.

Just when I sensed she couldn't take it any longer, I flicked her clitoris with the urgency she craved.

"It's coming, it's coming! My god, I'm coming," she screamed in desperate urgency. Then it seemed like a volcano burst, and hot liquid poured out spurts.

That ah girl.

My consolation prize from the most beautiful girl in Japan was the privilege to watch her shake into a stupor as her love juices poured into my mouth like a spout. Velvety remnants dripped onto the leather sofa, and I was jealous of the leather for absorbing what belonged to me.

In what seemed like superhuman strength, she pulled me by my arms, grabbed my dick, poised it over her wet center, then grabbed my ass and pulled me inside.

"Shit, girl…" I uttered, and she latched her lips onto mine, taking the rest of my pleasant thoughts into her breath. My mouth latched onto her breast, and my right hand went under her bottom. My left hand cradled her, giving her full access to every inch of me. "…you're gonna make me come too soon," I roared as her wetness poured onto my right hand.

Her pussy was a continuous spout as I pounded into her, matching the thrusts she made from below. I burst just as she contracted continuously while screaming for me to stop. She pushed me off her and used her right hand to milk me while directing the streams of cum towards her waiting mouth and breasts.

That visual pulled more nut out of my balls than I ever thought possible. I collapsed on top of her, spent. For the next few hours, I wrapped my arms around her and held her closer than close. I was completely shocked, satisfied, and amazed by what we had just shared.

Justine
Disgraced

I sat on the ledge of Mommy's all-white porch and watched the sun disappear into the horizon. The evening air chilled my bare arms. I felt as cold on the outside as I did inside. My plan took a detour, but I was determined not to let it foil altogether. Jacob had top security around him, keeping Destiny stowed away like she was fine china. Those kids hadn't been seen outside in at least a month. My mother and I were pretty much in the dark about the happenings in the Turner home.

Meanwhile, Montie was back in Atlanta, acting like a cocky asshole. He was supposed to have told the bitch everything, so we could all get our happily ever after. If he kept holding out, I was planning to pay him a visit in Atlanta like I did Destiny.

"It's a beautiful evening out, wouldn't you say, darling? How about we take a walk?" Mommy asked as she walked out onto the porch. Without waiting for my reply, she handed me a long-sleeve floral sweater and said, "Come on."

I hopped onto the foster green grass and put on the ugly sweater. I might as well walk off the nervous energy that had overtaken my being since I ran into Rick two weeks ago. He had the nerve to smirk in my face while trying to push up on me like I was a two-bit whore. I played along and seduced him into taking a ride out to Lake Pointe. At first, I genuinely wanted to spend time with him, reminiscing about what we once shared. I wanted to feel the way only Rick could make me feel. We laughed, talked, and everything was fine until the bastard dared to pull out his wallet and show me his new family—a beautiful, all-American-looking picture of his *wife* and kids.

A red glow covered him like a fog as he held that photo in his hand. I shut my eyes tightly and screamed internally. The fucking prick left me high and dry at the altar in front of a room full of people who showered me with pitiful looks. His actions led me into the arms of my best friend, who left me for another woman, breaking my heart all over again.

Then, Rick had to come back and rub his new life in my face right after screwing me in the back of his red Camaro. I showed him I was not the girl you played with twice. When I opened my eyes from snapping at him, I was a callous murderer. I left Rick in the back of his car with that precious picture of his family stuffed down his despicable throat that had been slit by my pocketknife. People should stop playing with my emotions. *I'm human too.*

Walking with Mommy was better than sitting around thinking about the shitty way people treated me and plotting revenge. I hoped the scenery of our neighborhood would deescalate my raging thoughts of men who'd claimed to love me. I didn't want Jacob to meet the same demise as Rick. I cared much deeper for him than I ever had for my "married fiancé," Rick...may he rot in hell.

"You're starting to get a little pudgy around your waist. You should come on these walks with me daily," Mommy said once we were thirty minutes into our power walk. My mind had been all over the place, thinking about Rick, Montie, and mostly Jacob. I merely responded to her questions with yes ma'am and no ma'am.

"Yes, ma'am."

"We've only done three miles out of the five we need to do. If you weren't moving like you had molasses in your heiney, we'd be finished by now," she complained.

"Yes, ma'am."

"I don't know how you ever think you'll get and keep any man with your weight fluctuating the way it does. Much less Jacob Turner. You have to have your body tight for a man like Jacob."

"Mommy, I don't need you telling me how to get Jacob. I'm going to marry him. You just wait and see."

She stopped walking. "Is that a fact?"

"It *is* a matter of fact," I assured her as I kept my pace. She jogged up beside me and turned me around to face her.

"And just how do you plan to pull that off when he has married Destiny?"

"That won't last long once Destiny finds out that Jacob and I slept together."

She glowered at me, disbelief written all over her hard features. I could tell she was skeptical of whether I was telling the truth because she tilted her head to the side and dissected me with her blood-sucking eyes.

"You slept with Jacob?" she asked with the beginnings of a smirk dancing on her cheeks. "Is that right?"

"A few weeks before he got married. Yes, I did."

"Why haven't you already blown up their world with this information? You could have sent Destiny on the Greyhound back to Atlanta long ago. Why are you withholding such damning information if you really slept with him and want to get him back? Help me understand what in the hell you are thinking."

"Mommy, it has to come out the right way. I can't just run over there and blurt that out to Destiny. She will never believe me."

"Well, did you record it or anything?"

"Mommy!"

"Don't Mommy me. I'm talking about gathering hard evidence that Jacob can't deny. He's a man, and he will deny sleeping with you. You had best believe that."

"I may have another way to prove it."

"What other way, honey?" I rubbed my stomach and her eyes bulged out of their sockets. "You are not."

"Yes, I am."

"Oh, my God. That's the ticket! There's no way he can deny it when you have his child in your stomach. Oh, my word Justie. You did it this time!" Mommy screamed excitedly and started walking faster than before, dragging me along by the arm. "Let's get home so we can tell your father that you're carrying the heir to the Turner Enterprise."

I wasn't as thrilled as she was about my pregnancy. I strolled behind her at a slow pace that caused her to stop and ask, "With such great news, what's wrong with you, Justie?"

"Nothing." I kept my eyes trained on the ground as we started back walking.

She stopped again. I could see a bile-rising disgust growing in her surly gray eyes. "You don't know who the father is, do you?"

I hung my head low.

She yanked her hand from mine, reared back, and slapped my jaw. "What a blasted disgrace! You'll never get married now. You're stupid to think a man of any respectable family will consider it." She stormed away from me, walking at high speed toward our house.

I sat on the curb and glanced into the wooded area in front of me. Ironically, I sat less than a mile from where I left Rick's dead body. I didn't need a husband. I needed help before I hurt someone else. My inner conscious pleaded with my mother's silhouette that moved further away from me until she disappeared into the house.

Lissa
Work Hard
Love Harder

"Do you have any more water in the fridge?" I asked Montie as I scooted to the edge of the bed. We had been sprawled out on his bed, testing the designs we were introduced to at the conference.

"Yep, there's some in there. Let me get it for you," he said, placing his hand on my waist to pull me down so I could sit between his legs in the center of the bed.

I swatted at his hands. "No, you lay down and let me get it this time. I know my way around your room by now, Montie."

"That you do, that you do," he said before his neck crooked, and his lips covered my nape.

I leaped from his grasp and scrambled to get to the edge of the bed. The chase was on as he pounced after me. He flipped me over so that I was underneath him. Overly eager lips sought

174

mine for a heated kiss. His hot, minty breath brushed against my face. "I see now that you're going to need some training," he murmured against my cheek as he flipped me onto my stomach and riddled my neck with a new avalanche of rough kisses. Montie yanked my shorts down to my knees and pulled my waist up, so it was suspended in the air. He quickly released his manhood through his boxers and thrust into my core without any other warning.

A gush of air flew from my lungs as I gripped the sheets. "Oweee!" I screamed as my dripping wet flower stretched to accommodate his size. "You can't just...can't just keep doing this to me," I admonished as I opened wide to let him in.

His hot breaths heated my neck as he hunched over me, pumping into my sex for dear life. Over and over, he stroked my hypersensitive core, from which more and more cream spilled.

"You're gonna let me take care of you, woman," he growled as he stroked me. "Do you understand what I'm saying to you? Damn, you're so wet! You gotta let me take care of you."

"Harder Montie, pump...harder," I said, surprised to hear my voice begging to be taken rougher. I could barely handle the full weight of his steel as he pulled all the way out to the tip and crammed it into my soft core without remorse. I thrust back against the length of his long dick until every nerve ending in my body came alive. Insurmountable sensations fluttered through my being, awakening parts of me that had been asleep all my life.

Montie's hand slipped between our bodies and flicked against my slit. Glorious vibrations rippled from the depths of my soul. I threw my heat toward him in a slow-rolling movement. Contractions rippled through my vagina and a forceful stream of cream released like jets. Montie jerked inside of me and his hot seed splashed against my walls, intermixing with mine.

"That was fireworks, baby," he said as I rolled over onto my side in a faint attempt to escape his grasp. "Don't make me light you up again for being disobedient," he said and playfully slapped my ass. He went to the refrigerator and brought back two bottles of water.

"If your intent is to get me to follow your command, maybe you shouldn't reward my bad behavior with good sex. Just saying." I accepted the water that I needed then more than before.

*****

The next morning, I lay in his arms, staring at the ceiling for hours before he was awakened by his alarm.

"How long have you been up?" he asked.

"Just a little while."

"Well, since I'm here, you're here, and he's here, I was thinking that we could maybe..." he pointed at the tent his manhood made under the covers. "...I don't know. What do you suggest we do?"

"I'm still sore from last night," I whined.

"Well, I'll let you rest for now, but I'm sure you'll need some type of punishment before the day is over with, sassy lady." He stretched before he stood and went into the bathroom, leaving me sitting up on the bed with my mouth hanging open.

"I'm beginning to believe you invited me along only so I can serve at your pleasure," I yelled behind him.

Montie peaked his head out the bathroom door. "No, that wasn't my intention, but now that you mention it, it's not such a bad idea," he said with one finger on his chin.

I bit down on my bottom lip as he approached the bed minutes later. His roasted brown skin was a perfect complexion I was convinced no other man could duplicate. His pectorals expanded from his chest, displaying the mighty strength that made it possible for him to suspend me in the air as he fucked me silly just before I fell asleep last night. I had, once again, attempted to get water to replenish the fluids he kept extracting from my body and found myself in a pleasurable "time out."

"Don't you want to get some water or something from the fridge?" Montie asked, standing over me, looking kingly.

"No, I don't want to get anything. Will you bring me a bottle of water, please?" I snickered.

"Smart woman. You learn pretty quickly." He turned around, swaggered to the refrigerator, and took out two water bottles. "You want juice or water?"

"I'll take an orange juice and water," I said, thinking it smart to have a stash for later.

He brought the two bottles and sat them on the bed beside me. He stood at the side of the bed and drank his juice. The adorable piece of meat hanging between his thighs jutted mere inches from my face. Halfway through drinking the bottle of juice, I screwed the top back on it and dropped it on the bed.

My cold hands reached for his manhood, and I began licking the tip. The bottle in his hand slipped to the floor as my mouth formed an O and sucked him in. He slowly pumped his awakening erection into my mouth. He threw his head back and murmured incoherent words as he enjoyed me pleasuring him. I salivated over every inch and didn't stop until I sent him to another planet.

Another round of mind-blowing sex and a nap later, Montie and I were up getting dressed for the conference. He caught me watching him buckle his belt around his waist. A silent conversation about whether we had time to make love again was exchanged between us: it was like a new addiction that neither of us had control over. His singing phone put an end to that tempting scheme.

"Hello," he kept his eyes on me as he answered on the second ring. A buzzing sound alerted him that the person had requested a video chat.

"Hey Montie, I'm glad you answered," a woman's voice rang out. "I have video of your son making the winning point for the All-Star championship!" she beamed. "I'm about to send it over now."

"My boy's a champ! I'm coming straight to Miami when I get back to the states," A huge smile spread across his face. I smiled just from seeing him so elated to discuss his son's game.

"He would love that. We'll plan a celebratory dinner for when you get here."

"Yeah, let's do that," Montie said, his eyes still trained on me. "I have someone that I want you to meet, and I'm bringing her with me."

"Oh...okay," his ex-wife stammered over her two-word answer. "On that note, getting together for that dinner is a must," she said.

"Yep," Montie walked over to me and took my hand into his. He brought it to his lips and kissed it. "A must."

"So, I'll send you the video when I hang up. It may take a little while to upload because it's long. I taped the whole game, so I might have to break it down into parts," she said.

"I can't wait to see it. I'll call Junior as soon as I get out of the conference. We're ten hours ahead here, but I want to congratulate my boy."

"Sounds great. He'll be glad to hear from you, Montie."

"Alright. Talk to you later." Montie hung up the phone and hugged me close to his chest. "My boy is a champ!" he repeated.

"Congratulations, Dad." I rested my head against his heart.

"I can't wait for you to meet my children. They are going to love you," he assured me.

"I want to meet your children too," I admitted, though I wondered if we were moving too fast. We had just made love, and I cared deeply for him. Why did I feel that it was too soon to meet his family?

"As soon as we get back to the states, that's where we're going," Montie said as he rushed into the bathroom and began shaving. His phone buzzed again, and he yelled, "Will you bring my phone in here? That's Destiny sending the video."

I swiped my finger across the screen to open the video, and a new call appeared on the screen. "I think you have another call coming in. I answered it by mistake," I acknowledged as a wild-eyed, white woman appeared on the screen. She began speaking as I rushed the phone to him in the bathroom.

I slowed to a standstill and listened to her rant.

"Montie, why have you been ignoring me?" she howled. "You just get what you want from me, and then you're out?" her voice blared into the room, filling it up with the painful feelings I knew so well.

The blond beauty with bewildered eyes went on about how Montie screwed her when he was in Miami and left her behind without so much as a follow-up call. I gulped in air and didn't release it. I shakily held the phone in my hand. I could no longer hear her words as I listened to what seemed like my experiences with Seth and Jameson warmed over.

"Who's that yelling on the phone?" Montie asked as he walked out of the bathroom, using a towel to dry his face. I raised my hand to stop him from coming close to me. He stood still and looked confused. "Who is it, baby?" he repeated.

"Who are you?" I questioned the irate woman.

"I'm the mother of Montie's unborn child, who will be on the next flight to Atlanta to kick your ass if he keeps ignoring me."

Bewilderment identical to Montie's grew in my own eyes. Surely, the woman was insane to think I would allow her to talk to me like that. "Excuse me?"

"You heard me right. I'm the mother of his unborn child. Therefore, I think the appropriate question is, who are you?" she hollered at the top of her lungs.

"Montie," I looked in his direction for an explanation for this confrontation.

He roared like an untamed beast as he pounced toward me to grab the phone. "Justine, what the hell is your problem? What kind of bullshit trick are you trying to pull now?"

"It's not bullshit. I'm saying I'm pregnant, and you may be the father."

"Justine, I protected us," he gritted out through clenched teeth. "There is no chance that you are pregnant by me."

"It wasn't enough protection because I'm pregnant."

"It's not like you hadn't been spreading yourself around before you fooled me into thinking you were someone else," he growled. "You're not carrying my child, so why are you calling me with this?"

I was stunned by how he talked to the woman and flabbergasted over what she accused him of. I would have started packing all my things out of his room to take to mine, but I was too amazed by the revelations to move.

"It's yours or Jacob's. I guess we'll find out when it's born." The woman sounded defeated.

"No, it won't be necessary to include me in any findings. If Jacob and I are the only two prospects, I'm sure you'll have a one hundred percent white child. We didn't conceive when we were together. I was extra careful." Montie ran his fingers over his dark, wavy hair and asserted, "It's impossible."

"Who is that woman, Montie? And what the fuck are you two talking about?" I screamed, unable to hold myself together any longer. There was no way the man who promised me he would be different than all the rest was standing in front of me, debating with a woman about being her baby's father.

"Who is *that* bitch that keeps talking, Montie, and why did she answer your phone?" Justine instigated.

"I'm not a bitch, but if you keep disrespecting me, I'll forget I'm a professional woman and introduce you to a bitch," I snatched the phone from Montie and yelled at her.

"Oh, I'm scared now, snowflake," she snapped back, placing her hand over her chest, feigning fear.

"I don't have time to play with children. I'm out of here, Montie." I picked up my clothes, sprawled across his hotel room floor and dressed as quickly as humanly possible. "You told me about everything except that you may have a baby on the way." I jerked my shorts over my hips. "I can't believe I trusted you."

"If I impregnated her, it would be the biggest mistake of my life, but it was before I met you, Lissa. I would never do anything to interfere with what we're developing. Believe me," Montie threw the phone down on the bed and came over to embrace me in a bear hug. "I can't let you walk out of here thinking that I disrespected you. I would never do that to you."

"If you tell Destiny about Jacob and I sleeping together, I'll have an abortion," the woman's voice blared through the phone again.

Montie stormed to pick it up. "Justine, this is part of your twisted plot to get Jacob back. I don't see the point of you calling to blackmail me about exposing that we slept together. I'm a grown man and have no problem saying what I did. You can tell Destiny about you and Jacob and about us. Just leave me the fuck out of your twisted plans to get back at Jacob!"

"I told you before it will be suspicious coming from me. Destiny trusts you," Justine whined.

"The mother of my children trusts me because I don't get involved in BS like this. Call me when you're ready to take a blood test, so you can get it through your head that there's no chance I'm the father of your child!" He hung up, took a deep breath, and walked over to stand in front of me. "Lissa, I fucked up, but it was before us," he explained.

"At this point, I don't want to hear any more about it. You should have told me about her when I was telling you all about my past or when you told me all about yours."

My mood grew darker than when he was on the phone with Justine. I had been determined not to repeat the mistakes that broke my heart to pieces. It seemed I had gone and done it anyway. Our fling was premature and out of bounds. I had to walk out the door and leave him behind. Experience taught me that these things don't end well for me. I had to cut my losses.

"Hear me out, Lissa."

"No, thank you. It's just the same warmed-over bullshit I've heard before. Goodbye, Montie." He reached for my arm to pull me to him, but I yanked away. "Just let me go, please."

Montie
Never Gonna Let Go

Lissa wouldn't so much as look at me the rest of the trip. She stayed in her hotel, refusing to talk to me. She closed me out completely, even changing her flight to ride back on separate planes so that I didn't know when she was leaving.

What in the hell was I going to do with this crazy woman saying she's pregnant and blaming the baby on me? Lissa would never again show me that wonderful blush of hers with those types of allegations swirling around.

"Mario, man, I had her right where I wanted her. Then, Justine calls with her fuckery," I explained to my friend. He was the only person I could talk to about the Justine bomb that had just landed in the center of my world.

"I know you said Justine is a cold piece of work, but that damn woman is a killer," Mario said.

"You just don't know the half of what you're saying."

"Oh yeah?" He leaned in, listening intently. "Say more."

185

"Listen, before I went to Japan, Destiny told me the police found this man named Rick, Justine's ex-fiancé's body, five miles away from her family's property. The police suspect foul play, and she's a prime suspect," I repeated the horrid details Destiny shared with me days ago.

Knowing I'd been in bed with a suspected killer caused a creepy feeling to crawl all over me. When I was desperate for one-night booty to rid my mind of Jacob and Destiny doting over each other, I hadn't been the best judge of character. How could I have been?

"She needs to be put down or put away. She's going to hurt someone else if she's not," Mario warned.

"That's what's so scary about her. She's lost touch with reality."

"Man, I say hop a plane and go handle her before she gets to your family."

"What do you want me to do? Go down there and kill her? I can't do that."

"I'm not saying to kill her, but something needs to be done."

"Taking her out is the only thing that will stop her. That or prison. She is way past sitting down and having a decent conversation. I just told you she's a suspect in the murder of her ex."

"I guess you have a point there."

"Of course, I do, Mr. "Stay Out the Way." Isn't that what you told me to do when I initially asked you how to handle it? Well, I stayed out of the way. Now, a deranged woman is running loose, ready to sink her claws into my children's mother, Lissa, me, Jacob, hell, maybe all of us."

"Call the Miami police and tell them your concerns. Tell them that you think she's the one that killed that Rick cat, too," Mario suggested.

"I thought about that. Maybe I will."

"So, what are you going to do about Lissa?"

"I have to figure out a way to get her to understand that I would never hide anything from her intentionally." I paused as my heart clunked against my chest wall. "I felt something genuine with her, something special. I'm not willing to get her involved any deeper in this Justine mess, though. I can't risk Justine trying to hurt her to get to me."

"That's understandable, but damn she's a beautiful woman. I'd hate to see her all alone with no one to keep her warm at night. But I'm sure you want the best for her, so I got you covered in that case. I'll keep her warm, bro…." Mario teased.

"If you touch one hair on my woman's head, you will find yourself in a world of danger. She's mine," I snarled in a voice that brooked no further jousting.

"You're so sensitive. Just kidding, man…dang."

"Well, I'm not. I'll get up with you later." I was done talking to him.

*****

After returning to the states, I called Lissa's office every day. She had assigned one of her designers to the new project

187

we were working on so she wouldn't have to speak with me directly. When I called to fuss about the change and demanded to see her face to face, she didn't answer her personal line. Her secretary said she was working from home. Since she wasn't answering her cell for me either, I finally took it into my own hands. Two days was far too long to be separated from her. I had to make her understand that I had good intentions for her.

On the drive to her home, I picked up the same salad she ordered when we ate at The Tavern and a bottle of her favorite wine. I parked and walked up to her front door. I heard voices on the side patio, so I paused just short of walking around the corner and listened to Lissa talk to her best friend.

"I want to see him so bad, but I think it's best if I just fade on out," said Lissa. A headwrap covered her naturally coily hair, and she wore no makeup. She had on an oversized t-shirt and slippers. Her creamy thighs glistened under the sunlight until she folded them underneath her.

"For him to look so well put together, he does have quite a bit of drama going on. The way you said that woman called and acted crazy reminded me of Rhonda. We both know what she's capable of." Shayla wasn't cutting me any slack.

"See, that's why I didn't want to fall for another man."

"Girl, when Rhonda told me she was pregnant with Titus' baby, I thought I would die. It felt like I got shot in the heart," Shayla said.

"Listening to Montie and Justine talk right before me wasn't too short of that. Another woman always slides into what I thought would be my spot."

"Lissa, you have to know that I would never hurt you," I turned the corner and my voice humbled as I laid eyes on her sad face.

"What are you doing here, eavesdropping on our conversation?" Shayla shuffled from her seat to her swollen feet to stand. Her protruding baby bump greeted me first.

"Shayla, do you mind if I talk to Lissa for a minute?" I asked.

"Yes, I do mind!" she yelled. "You can't just stroll up in here acting like you haven't broken my friend's heart. You lying piece of—"

"Please, wait for me inside," Lissa cut her off.

Shayla glared at me before she stormed inside the house, slamming the door behind her.

"Your minute starts now. Talk," Lissa said sternly.

I handed the salad over and placed the bottle of wine in the center of the table. "I'll never do to you what those other men did. I would never break your heart."

"And I'm supposed to believe that just because you said it?"

"Lissa, I have more to tell you. I just didn't want to tell you about her with us being so fresh into our relationship."

"Spit out what you have to say. You're down to thirty seconds now."

"Can I sit down beside you?"

"Sure." I sat beside her on the lounger. She whipped her head around and spit fire in my direction. "Fifteen seconds now, Montie. What is it that you couldn't tell me while you were standing?"

"This." I shifted on the chair, leaning down to forcibly crash my lips onto hers. I kissed her, my tongue exploring every morsel until I had her taste memorized. After just one kiss, I realized I would never have enough of this woman. Ever. There was no way I could let her go. But I knew that the first time our lips met. That's why I was there to plead my case for her heart.

Her hands reached up to grab the sides of my face. I could sense her pulling away, but she was too weak to resist. Her feeble moans in protest had no bearing over her tongue that caressed mine harder, deeper, and with increasing fervor.

An intense urge to be close to her, one with her—all that a man should be with a woman—overtook me. My hands ran wild with that urge.

"I can't do this...not out here...not with you. Sex won't fix the fact that another woman popped up saying you're the father of her child."

"Why not?" I murmured against her neck. "It was a one-night stand that didn't result in a child. Besides, you're mine. I can have you anywhere."

She pushed my chest with all the energy in her petite body. "Get off me, Montie. You can't come to my home claiming me when a woman is talking crazy on your phone about conspiracies, you having sex with her, and saying that she's pregnant with your child. I won't be made a spectacle of, not again. Nope. No, you're going to have to leave. I'm asking you to stop calling and coming by here."

"Lissa, you don't mean anything you're saying."

"Please respect that this is more than I can handle right now."

"I'm telling you that's not my child."

"And that may be true, but this ordeal has left me with a bad taste. It's enough that I have to deal with the fact that you were in love with your ex-wife up until a short while ago, but to know that you slept with her husband's ex and that she may be pregnant by you is pushing the bar of tolerance that any woman should have."

"I'll give you all of that and raise you one. I know for a fact the child isn't mine. I used protection each time I was with her and it didn't slip off or anything. Every drop of my sperm went down the toilet," I proclaimed.

"That's what every man whose being accused of being a baby daddy says."

"I'm a father, not a baby daddy."

"Humph," she shrugged her shoulders.

"Just say you're willing to end us because of a woman's *claim* that may be untrue, and what was meant to be our once-in-a-lifetime love dies a horrid death because of her lies. Will you be able to live with knowing that we'll never feel like this again?" I pulled her to her feet and cradled her in my arms.

She sighed deeply and allowed her soft body to fall onto mine. I palmed her hips and tugged her closer to me, so she was up against my ruggedness. Lissa didn't have to say the words her body spoke so eloquently to me. We stood there in silence, both knowing we didn't want to end like that.

191

Over the next few hours, I explained to Lissa and Shayla that Lissa was the only woman I cared for romantically. I told them about Justine attacking Destiny and that she was a treacherous witch who sought to destroy anyone in her path to Jacob. Shayla came around to my understanding and gave me her blessings with her best friend. Getting Shayla on my side was half the battle. She knew the power of outside deception in a relationship and told me a little about a woman named Rhonda that had tried to ruin her and her husband.

Lissa forgave me and asked me to spend the night. She said she didn't want to be alone. "Stay with me tonight," were four words just above a whisper that drew us back together.

We dressed for bed and just lay together. I fell asleep with her in my arms and it was hard to put on my shoes and walk out her door the next morning. A part of me wanted to stay for fear that leaving would erase our reconnection.

Montie
Win. Lose. Draw.

Destiny called me several times during the night but didn't leave a message. She hung up each time before I could answer and did not answer my return calls the next morning. Despite the stinging in my heart, I somehow managed to sleep a few hours, alerting me that trouble was looming.

I called Destiny once again on my drive home from Lissa's. Still, no answer. I got dressed for work and headed in. I used my key to open my office door and was shocked when three figures arose from my leather sofa.

"Surprise. Surprise, daddy, surprise!" Junior was the first to run over to me with his trophy in hand. "Look, daddy, I won. Daddy, daddy, my team won the All-State trophy, and we all got one to take home."

"I know you won, son. Your mother sent me the awesome video of you scoring the game point," Destiny had sent the video right after Justine's call. I sat lonely in my hotel room and watched it with hurt and pride flowing through me at once. "Give me a pound," I touched knuckles with my son. He jumped up in my arms and hugged me tightly. "I'm so, so proud of you, son. I'm glad that you won but very sorry I couldn't be there. I'll be there next time and that's a promise."

"It's okay, daddy."

Destiny stood there, gushing as Junior and I reunited. "Thanks for coming," I mouthed to her. She mouthed, "you're welcome" back.

"Well, had I known you guys were coming, I would have planned for a breakfast date," I said, scooping my daughter up and nuzzling up to her cheek. "I miss you so much, sweetheart."

"Miss you too, daddy," said Montana in her tiny raspy, toddler voice.

"Montie, I planned everything with Shalonda. We're your first meeting for today and she gave us a two-hour slot, so we can still go for breakfast. You know how much the kids love IHOP," she said and giggled.

"Oh, so Shalonda is just as sneaky as you are," I teased Destiny.

I caught up with my kids for a bit.

Destiny sat on the sofa and gave us time to bond.

"Who wants to go for some IHOP?" I asked them thirty minutes later.

"Ouuwee, IHOP!" Junior said and pumped his fist in the air. "Yes!"

"IHOP, yes!" Montana repeated happily.

Their excitement was undoubtedly due to Jacob's chefs cooking healthy foods for them every morning. Well, today, they were about to pig out on pancakes.

"Come on, I'll drive."

The conversation was light over breakfast. Destiny wasn't as talkative or nearly as cheerful as she normally was. Something was bothering her. "Are you okay, Destiny? You hardly said anything when we were at breakfast," I asked when we were back in my office lounging around.

"I'm fine," was her curt answer.

"The honeymoon must be over," I asked, knowing perfectly well that if Jacob cheated with Justine, he probably had changed into a jerk in other ways.

"No, everything is great, really," Destiny assured.

"Well, what's bothering you?" I prodded.

"It's just that Justine stuff with her ex being found murdered. That has been worrying me a lot, along with one more thing I haven't expressed to a soul, not even my mother. She's been traveling the world with John. I've hardly seen her since the wedding."

"Oh yeah. Your moms finally dug the right mine for gold."

"You just wait until I tell her you said that about her. She's going to get you."

"Tell her. She'll probably admit that it's partially true."

She chuckled.

I gave myself a pat on the back for being able to bring a smile to her face.

"Can the kids go sit with Shalonda while we talk?" she asked.

"Hold on." I picked up my phone and buzzed Shalonda's line.

"Hey, boss man."

"Got a request. Can Junior and Montana sit with you for a little while?"

"You'd better stop playing and bring my babies on up here," Shalonda responded before I could ask.

"Okay, thanks." I watched as Junior and Montana ambled up the hall and into Shalonda's waiting arms. I turned to Destiny, whose usual soft skin was wrinkled into a million worry lines. "Tell me what's on your mind, Destiny."

"Given our history, you may not be the ideal person to talk to about my problems, but you are still a good friend to me."

"We'll always be great friends," I agreed. Finally, I accepted our post-marriage relationship for what it would be—a friendship.

"So, tell me...what made you fall in love with me, Montie?"

I sat down on the sofa beside her. "Shit, that's a loaded question."

"What's your simple answer?" she asked, looking at me with the softest eyes and oozing her tender aura that kept me entrapped in the prospect of us getting back together for far too long.

"Everything about you, Destiny. From how you smile to how you rub your hair when you get nervous like you're doing now to how you look so innocent and caring at me. Everything. I loved everything." I spoke my fire-burning truth. I had loved that woman so long, so deeply, I thought I would never be able to rightfully love another.

She looked into my eyes and quickly looked away. If I hadn't seen it for myself, I wouldn't believe the burning passion emanating from her. "Montie, I guess I'm having second thoughts about how we ended things. With the kids being in Miami, I just wish that maybe Jacob and I would have stayed in Atlanta." Her words hit me in the gut.

"It would have been nice if you guys stayed in Atlanta," I said with the straightest face I could muster. It also would have been ideal if we had stayed married, but we're beyond that.

"If we would have stayed here," she continued, "then I wouldn't be in the same city as his ex, who always comes up in discussion when his mother is around. Jacob makes it clear that he doesn't want her around us, but his mother has an attachment to her, and it's excruciating for me to be around her. I'm getting to the point where I just want to move back. I'm tired of the entire charade of looking over my shoulder for the brutal woman that has an invite to my in-law's home. I told Jacob I'm uncomfortable, but he's been more subdued about her lately, like there's something more to them than before. He told me you ended up going out with her. How did that happen?" she rambled through a slew of thoughts, the final one I could have done without delving into.

"Oh, Jacob told you that?" I asked as my chest tightened into a huge knot over Jacob's audacity to put my business on front street without telling his own.

"Yeah, he said you guys hooked up when you were in Miami. Is she the reason you didn't come to the wedding?" she asked.

"No, I just didn't want to attend. Did Jacob also tell you that he slept with Justine in your new house?" It flew out in retaliation for Jacob's partial revelation of my truth. I clenched my jaw tight to suck the words back in. Saying them had been a pure reflexive reaction. I didn't mean to spill the beans like that. I truly didn't.

Destiny leaped from the sofa, doubling over and holding her belly. Tears sprang from her eyes, and a loud moan followed by a wail escaped her throat. "I knew it. I knew it," she repeated.

Montana rushed into the room and ran over to her mother. She rubbed Destiny's leg profusely as she tried to figure out what was wrong with her mother. "Mama, why crying?" Montana asked. "Why crying?"

"Mama, is something wrong with the baby?" Junior added, and my eyes nearly bucked out of their sockets.

Baby? Jacob got Destiny pregnant too?

"Are you pregnant?" I had to know.

She nodded and another cry sat repressed in her soul. I could see the pain bursting from her eyes, but she held it back. She didn't want to let go again in front of our children.

"Say goodbye to your father, kids. We're leaving," Destiny said, refusing to look at me.

I grabbed some Kleenex off my desk and wiped away her tears. "I'm sorry for blurting it out like that. I should've had more tact. I just don't understand why Jacob would tell you about me and Justine as if I would knowingly sleep with the woman that attacked you. I didn't even know it was her because she told me her name was Tracye."

More tears sprang a leak from her eyes. "I know you wouldn't hurt me, Montie. That's why I wanted to ask you face to face." She paused and the sting of my admission gamboled slowly over her features again. "He slept with her. The last time she was at his mother's house I left early. I didn't know what it was then, but now I know it was the vibes from her. Damn it, Montie! I left my life behind and moved into his world and he cheated on me. Got damn it!"

"Dammit," Montana innocently repeated to her mother.

"Jacob cheated on Mama," Junior said, working himself up so much that his tiny shoulders were heaving up and down.

Dang Montie. Great job, I thought as I scanned the room, looking at my distraught family.

As if things couldn't get any worse, Lissa walked through the door carrying a large bag of takeout and wearing a huge smile that instantly faded. "Hey, ba—by..." she sang as she stepped into the solemn room.

Destiny's eyes crashed into hers and flew to mine for understanding.

"Hey, honey," I held my hand out and pulled Lissa to my side. "Lissa, this is my ex-wife, Destiny. Destiny, Lissa is my girlfriend that I wanted to bring to Miami for everyone to meet."

Destiny's voice crackled as she greeted Lissa. "Ni-Nice to meet you."

"Hi, Destiny," Lissa said, then turned to me. "I stopped by to surprise you with lunch. I didn't know your kids would be here. I'll leave if you want me to," she said in response to the stunned faces of everyone in the room, including mine.

"No, baby, I want you to stay. You're not intruding," I assured her while gripping her hand into mine, unwilling to let her leave with any type of uncertainty of my alliance. I also needed her for strength to deal with the hurtful look in Destiny's red, puffy eyes. Her hand covering her stomach protectively didn't go unnoticed.

I walked Lissa over to introduce her to my children. "Kids, I have someone special that I want you to meet."

"I'll wait in the lobby," Destiny said softly. I raised a hand to halt her, but she bolted from the room, and I heard a series of whimpers as she trailed up the hallway.

"Look, Montie, I can leave. It won't be a problem, honey," Lissa inserted.

"It'll be a problem for me. I don't want you to leave, Lissa," I relayed. Destiny's reaction rattled me, but I pulled Lissa into my arms. "You're my woman, and I'm ready for you to be a part of my life and here it is. I will if I have to hold you like this until you stop saying you're leaving."

200

Cradled in my arms, she relented. "I'll stay. You can let me go now. The kids are watching," she said. "Hello, beautiful," she said to Montana, who looked up at her with big brown eyes.

"What's the matter, my mommy?" she asked, looking to Lissa for answers.

"Your mommy just needs a moment alone. She will be fine," I answered for her.

"Who are you?" Montana asked Lissa.

"I'm your dad's friend. What's your name?"

"I Tana," she replied.

"Well, hello, Tana."

"I don't know you," she said with her little fingers twiddling together.

"No, you don't know her, sweetheart, but I know you're going to love her as much as your daddy does once you get to know her," I assured my tiny princess.

"I lub daddy," Montana melted my heart as she jumped in my arms to claim her place.

"I love you too, Montana," I said, and a hearty smile spread across my face.

Junior stood watching the interaction between Lissa, Montana, and me. My mini-sized twin remained distant and uninterested in engaging us. "I'm going to the front with Mama," flew out of his mouth. He grabbed his trophy and ran to join his mother in the lobby.

"Junior, come back in here," I started after him, but Lissa stopped me.

"Let him go. This is a lot to process for a young boy who's obviously protective of his mother. You have to give him time to take this all in," she smartly acknowledged.

"Yeah, you may be right. There's a lot for everyone to take in today." I shifted Montana to my side. "Have a seat, and I'll be right back."

I took Montana into the lobby to find Destiny. She was on her cell, arguing with someone on the other end. "No, hell no. Don't come after me. I am not yours to tell what to do anymore. I'm moving back to Atlanta!" she screamed as she took Montana from my arms. "Come on, Junior. We're about to leave."

"Wait, wait a minute. So, you're just going to leave without talking to me?"

"What more is there to say, Montie? You just sprung on me that my husband slept with his ex a few weeks before getting married to me. The rest should be self-explanatory."

"That woman is obsessed with him, so she could have been lying to me. Make sure you talk to Jacob and give him a chance to explain himself," I pleaded.

"Oh, I just got off the phone with him. He admitted to everything."

My mouth fell open in shock. I couldn't believe Jacob had confessed.

She began pacing the length of the carpet. "He called me to tell me she'd been arrested for Rick's murder. When I told him I knew he slept with her, he came clean, saying it was the night the power was out and that he thought she was me."

I felt horrible for telling her the way I did. "I'm sorry it had to come out this way. It would have been better if Jacob had talked to you first. Getting duped by Justine and getting in the middle of you and Jacob's relationship isn't what I wanted. I apologize for blurting his indiscretions out how I did."

"I thought you would look out for me and tell me something like this *before* I married the man, not afterwards. But hell, it doesn't matter. Pretty soon, the tabloids will have a good story for all to laugh about!"

"Calm down, Destiny. Don't upset the kids any more than they already are," I said of a confused-looking Montana and an incensed Montie Jr.

Destiny rolled her eyes and frowned. "I'll see you later. Don't worry about my drama. Go back in there and talk to your *girlfriend."* She picked up her purse and stormed out with my children in her hands.

Lissa

The Burn in My Soul

Montie had knocked on my door an hour after I left his office. Now, he stood behind me, holding me in his embrace. I was a bundle of nerves as I spun around and placed a hand on his broad shoulder. Many thoughts swirled in my mind about Destiny's revelation that she was moving back to Atlanta. Would Montie be sucked back into her whirlwind of emotions and situations?

"Do you think we'll make it?" I asked.

"We can and will make it," he said confidently.

How could I tell him I was scared to death of letting him go but equally terrified of holding on and being hurt by him?

"What happened today with Destiny has me feeling uneasy," I said truthfully as he stroked my back. He eased his hands to the sides of my face and pulled me to him until our lips met. I stood on my toes and tried to bury my anxiety into his bated breath. "Kiss me like that again, and I'll forget all my worries," I admitted.

"You don't have a damn thing to worry about where I'm concerned, woman."

My heart fluttered as I walked away from him. I had some things to get clear. Being subjected to his kisses wouldn't help. Montie told me that Destiny was emotional about finding out about her husband's alleged affair, but her face when he introduced me still troubled me. She was going through it, but when Montie introduced me as his girlfriend she crumpled right before my eyes.

"You've been pulling away from me since you met my family today."

"Your family? No, I had no problem meeting your children. It was your ex-wife that gave me bad vibes." I wasn't going to say anything to Montie about it, but I just put it out there. If we were going to have anything meaningful, I had to be honest with him and myself about how I felt.

"I told you she was upset because she found out about me and Justine and then I told her about Jacob sleeping with Justine," he reiterated.

"I get that, but when you introduced me as your girlfriend, instant devastation overtook her. It didn't appear that she was already upset about something, and it was continuing. She got hurt deeply upon hearing your acknowledgment of me."

"I can't imagine that upsetting her, given that she's already married another man." Montie shook his head. "Even if I agree that your assessment is spot on, it doesn't matter if Destiny is hurt over me finding everything I could ever want and need in a woman. I thank the heavens every day that I found you, girl." His fingers ruffled my hair and traveled to my face, sending warmth through my body.

Montie placed loose hair strands behind my ear that had been in my face hiding the anxiety in my eyes. He pulled me into a warm hug, clutching me close to his chest. I sucked in everything Montie. He always smelled so good. The peace I found in his capable arms circumvented the uncertainty that shook me to the core earlier with Destiny.

"I love you, Lissa," he said as he held me in his arms.

"That's the part that hurts, knowing that I love you too and thinking that another woman has the power to end us."

He held my face so that I was looking him dead in the eye. "I want you to know that no one has the power to end us but us," he pointed between us. "I hate that our beginning has been rapt with drama. I can promise you that you are the one and only woman that has my heart."

"But you slept with Justine while Destiny had your heart."

"I wasn't in a relationship with Destiny at the time, and I did it to distract me from the burning rejection from my ex-wife. I was in denial that we were truly over, but we were, and I have never been deceitful to her when we were together. I'm a one woman's man."

I cut him off before he could continue. "That's what I'm saying. It's only been a few months since you didn't know if you could stand to live without Destiny. How can you be sure that you're over her?"

"Because if I weren't over her, I could never do this." He sucked my bottom lip into his mouth and kissed me deeply. He released a drawn-out groan into my mouth. As he methodically moved his tongue against mine, his warm hands slipped around my waist and settled atop my plush bottom before he began to unbutton my dress. "If I were still feeling her, I could never—"

"Montie, I'm serious. We have to talk about this."

"Oh, I'm serious as a heart attack, Lissa. I could never kiss you and feel it burning in my soul if you didn't have my heart. Love is an action word for me. There is no woman, and I repeat, no woman that moves me the way you do. What Destiny and I had died a long, slow death, but it's dead. You rescued me from hell on earth. I'll be damned if I let the same person who pulled me into that abyss drive you away from me."

"I'm not running away. I'm just extra careful with my heart." She blew out a warm breath that I eagerly sucked in.

"That makes two of us." Forehead to forehead, I asked, "Do you remember when you asked me if I trusted you?"

"Yes."

"Well, I'm asking you now to trust me."

Staring into his sincere brown eyes, I said, "I trust you."

"Turn around."

"Why?"

"I thought you trusted me."

I turned slowly.

He pressed his body against mine. His prominent erection pressed against my ass. My head fell back against his chest. I felt his body heat collide with mine for a few moments. Montie bent me over and slipped my panties down. He fumbled with his belt and took his erection in his hand before cramming it into my tight heat.

I was his, body and soul, as I begged for mercy. For the time being, the joining of our bodies convinced my mind that held so many memories of heartbreak to come along for the ride.

SIX MONTHS LATER
Montie
This Love of Ours

"This is your last goodbye," I said, stepping up to claim my woman. "Destiny's good without you, man. I got this covered," I pushed the door to the home Destiny and I built closed in Jacob's face. But he thrust the door open and pushed me backwards.

"The hell you mean she's good? Man, if you don't get out of my face there will be problems for you. You have gotten in the way enough, Montie."

I scowled at Jacob, ready to pounce at any moment. "If you know what's good for you, you'd get out of here," I roared as I spoke. Mounted up in his face so close that spittle flew from my mouth and landed on him, I growled. Fire flew from my nostrils as I tried to breathe to get my temper in check. The maneuver was futile. Before I knew anything, I had my hands all over him, pushing him back over the threshold. "Don't come back to my woman's house. It's over...."

"I am not leaving here until Destiny tells me what you are doing here," he retorted, barging past me and into the foyer. "Is there something else you should tell me, Destiny? Is he the real reason you gave back my ring?" he asked Destiny, and I waited for her to tell him the truth. When she didn't answer, I spoke up.

"Get out of this house!" I pushed Jacob toward the door. He struggled to stay inside, but he didn't put up much of a fight. He obviously was waiting on Destiny to defend their love, which I was sure had ended.

"I'm warning you to keep your hands off me, Montie," Jacob said as his eyes traveled to mine. "She's not unconscious anymore, so she can speak for herself."

"She sure can. Tell him to take his ring and get out of here, Destiny! He's clearly hard of hearing." I raged toward her and stood face to face with the woman who seemed incapable of defending my honor. "Tell him, Destiny." I stopped short of pleading with her.

"Montie, I can handle it!" she said and moved away from me.

And Destiny did handle it. She tossed me out and allowed Jacob back in. I never thought I would be able to view that day in a good way until I was blessed with the sight of Lissa McDaniel's smile.

As I drove her to what she thought was just another business meeting, her face confirmed that she was sent into my life to be my peace in the storm. My worst day set up the best day of my life. The day I would ask the woman who was the glue to my broken heart to be my wife.

Justine was sentenced to twenty-five years in the murder of her ex. DNA evidence and her lipstick being found on the scene were the nails in her coffin. I waited six months for her to produce the child she claimed to be three months pregnant with when she revealed it to me. According to the prison, she wasn't even pregnant to begin with.

Destiny moved back to Atlanta, giving me more time with my children. It hurt me to see her so sad about Jacob's cheating. As a friend and father of our children, I did everything in my power to cheer her up. I took the kids more often than on weekends, which Lissa loved. I figured giving Destiny time to heal without having to be the caregiver to our children was what she needed most from me.

A few times, when I came over to pick up the children, I saw Jacob staked out in front of her house. He'd get out and jog up to the door behind me, hoping she would talk to him. She always slammed the door in his face without giving him a chance. He told me the story about how Justine tricked him into thinking he was making love to Destiny. I don't know why, but I believed him and prayed that he would be able to get through to Destiny. Now that my heart wasn't intertwined in their relationship, I could admit that I understood their love for each other. An even deeper burning desire for Lissa lived in me.

I pulled into a parking space at Holistic Medical and hopped out. I opened the door for Lissa. "Honey, this is everything I've ever dreamed of. We'll go in here and make the biggest deal of our lives. I hope you're ready to have the world at your fingertips," I said.

She picked up her briefcase and strode beside me confidently. "I'm ready for it all. We deserve this."

We entered the building and went to Mr. Bromage's office. Indeed, we signed a five-million-dollar deal to design exclusive medical software that would be distributed to all Holistic Medical offices and their parent company. When the contracts were signed, Mr. Bromage asked if we could go into the testing area and look at a glitch he had encountered. "I have it loaded on this computer, so I can show you the real problems we're having," he said, pointing to the computer in the center of the room.

I pulled the chair back for Lissa to sit down and she moved the mouse. The screen saver had the word "WILL" in all caps, but the screen would not change over.

One by one, workers from Holistic Medical walked in with shirts that read: YOU. MAKE. ME. THE. HAPPIEST. MAN. ALIVE. AND. MARRY. ME. LISSA?

When she realized what was happening, she turned to me and I was on one knee.

"Lissa, I love the way you handle the less fortunate. It's exemplary of how you handle my heart, which was so depleted when I met you. Your past roughened you around the edges, so you didn't even know what to think of our relationship back then. I'm just glad I could capture the beautiful passion within you and bring it out for you to enjoy again. We deserve to relish the spoils of our love for the rest of our lives. We are the example of a power couple because we powered each other up...rebooted the love we both tried to bury within. So today, I'm asking will you, many years from now, still handle my heart with care that restores it? Will you, in years to come, allow me to live to bring that beautiful smile to your face? Lissa, will you marry me?"

Her head nodded vigorously as tears flowed from her eyes. I stood and kissed each tear away.

"Yes! I will marry you, Montie. I will marry you," she exhaled as the room erupted in sniffles, applause, and yells.

THE END

To get updates on my new releases, join my mailing list.

Join Us! Shani's Imperial Reading Group is accepting new members. We have a blast talking about books, sharing quotes and hunks like Tobin, and hosting giveaways.
Don't miss out on the fun!
~Shani

Breathless

IN LOVE WITH AN ALPHA BILLIONAIRE

5

A BWWM ROMANCE BY

SHANI GREENE-DOWDELL

Breathless 5, Loving Jacob is available now!

Destiny

Loving Jacob is easy. Gazing into his eyes, I melt like heated butter. Our chance meeting so many months ago has produced a love like no other, including the sole heir to Turner Enterprises and his firstborn. With our child on the way, I should be the happiest woman alive. And I am until Justine drops a bombshell about her pregnancy. It's an uphill battle to give Jacob the same redemption he gave to me when another woman's bombs just keep on dropping in the center of our love.

Jacob

Feeling our baby's bump in the palm of my hands, I know one thing. Destiny holds the key to my heart. She belongs to me. There's no way I will ever let her go. Yet, a dark cloud hangs over us from a mistake I made. A slip-up I kick myself for every morning I arise from bed. My only hope is that Justine digs deep within herself to find a shred of decency to put Destiny's heartache to rest. Destiny can't walk out on the love we made. There are no if, and, buts, or maybes about it. I was made to love her, and she was made to love me—until the end of time.

Breathless 5 is a BWWM story of redemption and rekindled love. It features a hot, rich, powerful alpha male who isn't afraid to bare his heart and soul to the woman he loves. This installment ends with a happily ever after.

Continue to book 5 in the Breathless Series